MONSTERS' CREW

EVERNIGHT PUBLISHING ®

www.evernightpublishing.com

Copyright© 2021

Sam Crescent

Editor: Audrey Bobak

Cover Art: Jay Aheer

ISBN: 978-0-3695-0298-8

MONSTERS' CREW

MONSTERS' CREW

Crude Hill High, 1

Sam Crescent

Copyright © 2021

Chapter One

Emily

I thought about death a lot. It wasn't morbid or for some quest to finally find the end. At eighteen years old, I hadn't really lived. There had to be more to life than this empty shell of nothing. Life seemed to be playing out, and the longer I was part of it, the less I seemed to be relevant. I didn't fit in. I wasn't part of any crowd. To most, I was a loser. I didn't mind. It helped me to dwell in my thoughts of death. For all I knew, a lot of kids thought of dying. About how their final moments on this very earth were going to go.

Glancing around the cafeteria, I couldn't help but wonder if that wasn't a whole crock of shit. The pretty girls. All with their long hair, styled pretty much the same, but there was always one girl who liked to change it up. For the team here, it was Nancy. She ran with the pack but the truth was, she danced above them all.

Then, of course, around them were the jocks. The football crew who believed they ruled the entire school, but the truth was they weren't in charge, not really. I'd firsthand seen them really bowing down to one group of people, and they sat in the corner. No one messed with them.

Monsters' Crew or the Monsters' Boys. Depending on who you spoke to. Caleb Falls, River Block, Gael Parson, and finally, Vadik Keller. All of them deadly. No one crossed them. Even now as I glanced at them, I saw River with a knife between his fingers. He flicked the blade back and forth as if it was nothing more than a pencil. I'd seen him do this many times and yes, he'd even nicked himself, but he'd often just lick it up or wipe the blood away on his pants.

They were all scary as fuck. Caleb, their leader, made all the decisions. He always took the helm and the other three surrounded him, protecting him. Black hair, blue eyes, and he never smiled. It was odd to think about. He never laughed. When he found a target, he'd get this weird look on his face that vaguely resembled a smile, but it never was.

Taking a large bite of my burger, I averted my gaze as Caleb looked right at me. The last thing I wanted to do was to catch their attention. Everyone knew what happened if you caught their attention.

The girls loved it. I'd heard the rumors of the boys tag-teaming girls and then discarding them. A couple had left the school as they spent way too much time sobbing about the fact they couldn't win one of them over. They were Monsters and were more than happy to wear the label as well.

Out of some of the guys who wished to join them,

a couple of them had never been seen or heard from again. To the outside world, this was a prestigious school. Wealthy kids came here. All of the Monsters came from money. They were all filthy rich, but no one here was from the squeaky-clean kind of group. Nope.

My parents dealt in sordid deals and blackmail. They owned an entire city, and I'd even caught conversations about trafficking. There had been a lot of young women coming in and out of their house. Most of them covered in bruises.

I hated it.

There was nothing I could do about it. This school was the one place where I could breathe without worrying someone was watching. Of course, they *were* watching. Even the jocks, they came from backgrounds that had a double-edged sword.

I grew up surrounded by competition and the enemy.

Slurping up my banana milkshake, I jumped, nearly choking on the straw at the sound of a loud clattering.

Near the Monsters' table stood a kid I didn't recognize. He was clearly a year, or several years, below us.

River got to his feet and the tension in the room mounted. Silence fell.

"Please, no, please." The boy's whimpering filled the air.

The biggest mistake he could make.

In hell, no one ever showed weakness. We were all monsters, all destined for lives we didn't want. At the top of the tree stood the four Monsters, and we were nothing but their minions. I hated it.

River slammed the kid to the table. The blade pressed against the boy's throat.

"You think it's funny to throw a spitball?" River asked.

See? All of this over a wayward spitball that had come at the beginning of the school day.

Nibbling on my lip, I watched as the boy held his hands up in surrender. He was in the wrong place and was about to become target number one in a sea of sharks. I'd seen enough as River landed the first blow. As if on cue, Caleb, Gael, and Vadik got to their feet, and away they went. Anyone who dared to step up would feel his wrath.

With my tray in hand, I dumped the trash into the bin and left the dining room. My heart pounded.

Violence disgusted and fascinated me in equal measure. I hated myself for it. There was no way for me to get away from it.

The marks on my back were already evidence of my absolute hatred of it. My father wasn't known for his patience and since I was his only daughter, he always made an example of me. Unlike my brother, who was always considered the best thing in the Crane household.

Stepping out into the cold day, I stayed perfectly still.

Would dying from being left in the cold be so bad? In the movies, it never looked painful. I'd rather go out with no pain than to be screaming.

After a few seconds of stillness, I moved, heading toward my next lesson. There were five minutes of lunch left. Teachers rushed past me and I stepped out of their way. The last thing I wanted to do was step in their path. They had a boy to save.

This was what you got at Crude Hill High. There was a time it was a boarding school for our very kind, but there was too much death, leaving the families no choice but to keep the gates open.

On rare occasions, the gates would be locked and it was like a free-for-all. Two years ago, that had happened. Someone had broken the rules and brought a gun. That had ended messy. Mom tried to persuade my dad to send me elsewhere. To let me have a normal life.

No Crane was normal.

We were sharks, thriving to be on top.

The truth was my father craved a place at the four. He wanted to be the fifth shark, but with what I knew, he didn't have the balls to do what these guys did.

I arrived at English, taking a seat in the back near the window. School sucked. It was boring. Teachers tried to pretend we were like other kids. The ones who weren't going to be responsible for killing people when we got out of here, but no matter what they tried to tell themselves, it was never going to happen.

We were the enemy. Plain and simple, and if one of them stepped out of line, their lives would be forfeit. It was hard for a teacher to threaten you when you could have them killed at a snap of your fingers. The cops were useless here, so was security footage. Money talked and the more you had, the better it was for you.

My family was wealthy and throughout the years, I'd learned how to take care of myself. I had to. Without it, I'd have been dead in the water long ago.

The English teacher came in. It was Mr. Bucati, who had replaced the previous teacher two years ago. The one before him had been caught sleeping with a student, and seeing as he was supposed to be teaching all the fine arts of literature, and the girl in question was supposed to remain a virgin until her precious wedding night, the previous English teacher was now lying dead in an unmarked grave, at the bottom of the lake, or just plain dead. No one knew, and the girl had also disappeared. This was another precious little detail in our world. We weren't just shipped off to some foreign place until the scandal died down. Nope, sometimes the girls or the guys were never seen or heard from again.

Keeping your nose clean was more important in this world.

I licked my dry lips, keeping a close eye on the door as one by one, students filed in. To the outside world, we were set up like every other school. Like in the cafeteria, jocks, cheerleaders, the rebels, the nerds, and me, the loner. But the truth was, lower your guard for even a second, and we were all dead.

It was odd to think how many of us actually went here. I don't have an exact number, but we filled a rather prestigious school. The crooks' kids. Criminals. Taking over from our families when the time was right.

Since I was a female, my only role, according to my dad, was to get my education so I could marry. I was sure he already had a man who I would hate lined up. Unlike some of the more exclusive mafia types who liked to keep their daughters virginal and completely cut off from the rest of the world, there were those who wanted us to be prepared. For my dad, I was potentially a spy. With a daughter in high school, right in the middle, he could find out who was who. It gave him an excuse to come to my parent-teacher nights. Those were fucking fake. I knew he was fucking my art teacher. I was shit at drawing or painting, but yet, it was a subject I had to take. My mom never came to my parent-teacher nights. She always had to stay home.

Father's rules.

I hated him more than I hated anything else. If I had the courage to do one thing in my miserable life, it would be to take a blade to his fucking neck, slice him open, and watch as the blood leaked from his useless, pathetic body. He was a scary piece of shit.

All of our families were. There were rarely any coward's kids, but it did happen. There were bastard kids as well. Drake, one of those kinds of kids, came in. He had short hair, a torn shirt, and ink completely covered his arms. He took one look at Bucati and went in for a pretend attack.

Bucati was used to this and didn't even flinch. On the first day, he did and went running to the principal. From that day forward, he had to learn to grow a spine. I imagined the teachers here got paid a fortune. Money always changed hands when they were told to look the other way.

Drake dropped down into a chair, spreading his legs out. He was the bastard of one of the English family's gangs. His father owned part of London or something, and he was the one who kept the streets clean. Drake was a loose cannon. Rumor had it he came from a rapist father, and he wasn't used to being told no.

He was one of the few guys I steered well away from. Catching him on a bad day led to bad things.

The activity in the room paused. There was no need for me to see who had actually entered. For all of Drake's craziness, it didn't take the whole Monster Crew to create tension. It only needed one, and right now, Caleb Falls had entered the classroom.

The girls were all fawning over him. Me, I stayed perfectly still, used to keeping to myself. It was the only way to survive in hell.

****

Caleb

"Dude, Bucati is a pussy. You remember what happened to him on the first day of school?" River asked. He bent down, grabbed a stone, and launched it across the parking lot toward the English teacher.

I smirked. There was nothing else to do.

Watching Bucati wander the school halls as if he was better than all of us pissed me off. It got on all of our nerves. Mr. English could keep his dick in his pants, but I'd been present when my father finally decided to pay a visit, and it hadn't been pretty. Bucati pissed himself. Begged for his life. Then actually got down on his hands and knees and offered his body for personal use. Anything. My father had turned to me and told me this was what weak looked like.

I'd never forget it.

Since then, Bucati was paid, not well. The other teachers made sure they got a good deal out of it. Every now and then, he'd turn up at my father's house to do what needed to be done. If it was a deal that needed to be sealed with a nice fuck, Bucati was there.

I didn't like him.

Bucati acted the part of authority, like he was above all of us, but I saw the way he looked at some of the girls who came to this school. While my father believed he had Bucati made, I knew men like him would use an opportunity to screw up a bigger deal. Virginal girls were still a huge prize in our world. Unlike the exclusive, keep-it-in-the-family mafia, who didn't frequent this school, our girls were still expected to act the part most of the time.

Some of the girls who went here were just pawns in their fathers' lives. They had no chance of going up in the world, just down.

Getting laid was easy. There were many willing females. Some students, even teachers. I think Gael was the one to prove that a married civilian woman's love meant nothing. A sweet little scientist had come to the school a few months ago, flashing her ring, again, looking rather smug. All it had taken were a few choice words from Gael, and she'd been bent over her desk, begging for his cock to be driven into her ass. For added proof and I was guessing pleasure, Gael had filmed the entire thing. Once he was done with her, he'd made her lick his cock squeaky clean and then smile at the camera.

It was what Gael liked to do. If there was ever a job that required toying with someone, he was always the first one in line.

"I'm not interested in throwing stones at people." I jumped off the wall and headed to my car. Another gift from my father for a job well done. Where most of the people who went to Crude Hill High were still trying to prove themselves to their respective families, to earn their part, I had my place. I had the ink making me part of the Monsters' Crew. All four of us had earned our spot.

At eighteen years old, I already had a body count of over ten. I had no feelings when it came to people.

My father liked to test me. Had even gotten me to kill a woman who had betrayed the crew. It was what we did. We owned cities, people, and we made sure everyone knew who they were dealing with.

Apart, we were all deadly, but bringing us together, we were the worst fucking enemy, and what was also rare, all of us were in high school at the same time. Our fathers had knocked up our mothers, and they'd all been pregnant at the same time. It was why our bond was so strong. From the time we were first born, all four of us had been pushed together. Without a doubt, I knew the only people I could trust were right in this room, and that was all I needed. There was no reason to rely on anyone else.

The only people I needed were right here and now.

Movement out of the corner of my eye caught my

attention.

Emily Crane walked out of the school gates. Like all the times before, her gaze was focused around her. She was the only person in the entire school who didn't have a whole host of friends swarming around her. Fitting in clearly didn't appeal to her. She wasn't part of any clique. She made no friends.

With her arms weighed down by books, she headed toward a blackened-out car. A large man, a security guard, got out and held the door open for her. He tried to take the books but she dodged him, climbing into the car without another look at him.

Shaking my head, I smiled.

This school was never boring, with all this entertainment.

Crane was a well-respected man. Even my father talked about him highly. He was known for getting shit done and killing anyone who failed him. For anyone to get respect from my dad, it meant bad things happened a lot.

"I always think she's a bit strange," River said, climbing into the car, holding a knife in his hand. No matter where we went or what we did, he always held a knife. Today, he'd gone for a little pocketknife.

I knew him well. It would be one of the sharpest. School or not, he carried a weapon. Not that Crude Hill High was a safe place. Nope. People died. Enemies' kids were sent there. It was a breeding ground for pain and violence. I liked it.

I didn't have to hide away if I was there, and I never backed down from a fight. Even if there was one I knew I wasn't going to win. Being a Monster didn't mean I was invincible.

We'd all lost a fight. The difference between us and everyone else was we didn't cower or hide. We came back for more. We may lose once, but the next time, our opponent would end up dead.

As I turned over the ignition, my beauty purred to life, and I pulled out of the parking lot. All the fancy houses were nothing more than a cover. Employees and staff lived here. There were a few civilians, but for the most part, every person who lived in Crude Hill knew what was coming to them. The police department was a joke.

If someone called for an emergency, there was no cop to come and help. They had two lines. The line to the outside world, and a constant call to whoever had the deepest pocket. This town was our own personal playground, and what was more, every single family here could make sure no press ever made it close to the school or to the town. Some kids thought they had it rough. They didn't know anything. Not here.

"I want to get my dick sucked. You think Meg's is open?" Gael asked.

Meg's was a massage parlor. It was run by one of the southern crime lord's mistresses. So far, Meg wasn't up for sale, but it would only be a matter of time before her pussy went on the market.

Mistresses were crème de la crème. A lot of men tended to open up about shit once they'd come, and mistresses were great stress relievers. Of course, in most cases, said mistress was kept away from the wife.

I smiled, remembering when my dad actually brought his mistress home. He'd wanted her to become a nanny, even though there were no young kids. My mom went completely crazy. The mistress didn't last the night. In our world, our women, unless they were trained properly, they were just as violent as the men. My dad liked my mom crazy. He liked her drawing blood, fighting for him. Sometimes, I didn't even believe he fucked around on her, he just liked to use her to get his kicks.

Strong women were rare. For as many who had a backbone and could shoot their husband down, I'd also witnessed those who slowly succumbed to the numbness of pills and drink. This wasn't an easy life for anyone. It was hard, painful, and not in the least bit fun.

"It's Vadik's turn to say what we're doing," I said, looking toward the back.

Vadik smirked. No one ever liked what he wanted to do. Where all of us embraced our life, Vadik made sure we had some time where we were actually eighteen-year-olds. He wasn't weak. No, to cross him got you killed. I'd seen how he fought, and his loyalty was to us four. Not to his father, or our combined fathers, but to us. One day, all four of us would take over, and it would be us running things. Until then, he kept us balanced.

Which was why, an hour later, with burgers and fries, we sat in the movie theater, watching some action film.

Gael would be pissed, but he liked to just relax as well.

River always took the opportunity to sleep. Watching a movie, with the three of us guarding his back, it was roughly the only time he relaxed. The Block family had a lot of enemies. River hadn't been the same since he was taken for three days when he was sixteen years old. Mistakes had been made, and River paid the price. Half of the scars on his body were from that time. Three days could kill a person. It had messed River up and it meant he spent a great deal of time training. He got cut up really bad, and it was what had created his fascination with knives.

No one would ever be able to get the drop on him. For hours, we'd sit around a junkyard as River threw blade after blade at a target. Not once would he stop until every single knife he threw hit its target.

This made him feel safe.

Vadik nudged my shoulder. "Word is out that some pimps got through security and are patrolling the grounds, waiting for the opportunity to strike. My dad gave me the warning. It's an immediate kill. Don't ask questions." He held up his cell phone, and I looked at the men.

I nodded. When River woke up, he'd be given the update. Gael waved his hand, letting us know he heard.

Taking a bite of my burger, I leaned back, but it wasn't the movie I watched. No, for some strange reason, I thought about Emily Crane.

My dad had told me to watch my back, to keep an eye out. He wanted to know of any proposed marriages to her, or if she gave even a hint of what her father was like. So far, nothing. I'd known her since kindergarten. Always kept to herself. Like most of us, she had bruises on rare occasions.

There was no reason for us to question where they came from. It was like how one of us could come in with a broken bone. Everyone would know why, but nothing would be done.

To many, we were the scum of civilization. But the truth was we were the fucking kings of the underground. The monsters people were afraid of, and everyone had offspring, even those that people wished just faded into nothing. My father was responsible for a lot of pain and suffering. His name came with a sneer attached, and what was more, he embraced it. As he'd told me, fear is power, and if I didn't learn to harness it, I was worth nothing to him. What I had to do was prove myself.

All of us had proven what we were capable of.

Each of us had a nickname. I was known as the bogeyman. I had no feelings and I struck where it hurt the most.

I liked my nickname, and I intended to live up to every single letter of it.

Chapter Two

Vadik

I hated school.

It was the single most annoying part of my life. This was pointless. I got the only education I needed at home. I wasn't stupid. I didn't need to know history or physical education. Dribbling a ball didn't appeal to me. Training, math, and English, that was all I needed to take over from my father. That, and the ability to take a beating.

That was one of the first rules I was taught from the moment I turned twelve. No man in the Keller line would ever be a wimp. We had to be able to take a beating, to not break, and so, on weekends, he tortured his son. He made me the man I was today, hungry and desperate for the chance to get the hell out of here.

Yes, this was hell, but I relished it. The pointlessness of it all. The only thing I lived for was when one of these pieces of shit thought they could take us. Then the real fun happened. But learning, giggling girls, I hated it. Real lessons came in power, in fear.

Right now, Lauren was the current irritation on my never-ending list. Gael had her sitting on his lap, his hand beneath her skirt. If she didn't shut up, I was going to cause a war. She wanted to get all of us between her thighs. Lauren was a low, which meant her family wasn't powerful. They had some money, but it was handed down. They had enough to get into this school, but nothing more. Their sons or daughters were often sent to snag a rich man or a position near someone like me.

Lauren was trying to find anyone who would give her a good life. She was useless. There was no power there, and her giggle pissed me off. It was fake.

I couldn't stand fake people. I'd rather kill them.

"I bet you'd let me fuck you right here, wouldn't you?" Gael asked.

"Not while I'm eating," Caleb said.

River snorted. "Like it would matter. She is just hungry for cock. Any cock that has enough money to keep her in a good life."

Gael had thrown the test down, and Lauren hadn't passed. He dropped her to the floor as if she was nothing and turned his back to her. The women only got one chance, and if the guys didn't want her, she was done for.

Lauren had been passed around by so many of the guys. She was known for being easy, and now she had tried her shot at the Monsters' table and wasn't up to scratch. The rumors about us always ran wild. I liked them. Not talking too much gave me an edge. Talking made shit worse and in our world, being quiet saved your ass. At least, most often, it saved my ass.

People didn't exactly know how we ran things. We were a unit. We played with women, and on occasion, we shared them. There was nothing more satisfying than watching a woman beg for all of us, to pass her boundaries and to actually attempt to win us over.

Women of all ages had tried.

None of them had kept our attention.

Commotion in the cafeteria line caught my attention.

Drake was there as he always was, causing shit. He'd picked up the tray of lasagna and threw it across the cafeteria. Next, he jumped across the counter, grabbed the guy who served, and started to bash his head against the glass.

Security was on their way. Drake was making a nuisance of himself. So long as he left us alone, I didn't give a shit, but we liked peace and quiet at lunch unless we were the ones giving out the pain.

Out of the corner of my eye, I spotted her. Emily Crane. It was hard to miss her. Long blonde hair, full, red lips, beautiful, with green eyes that should only look at rainbows and flowers. When I took the time to look at her, I saw pain. I saw something else, acceptance. She knew who she was, what we were, and what she needed to do.

I flicked my tongue across my lip.

The uniform the girls were forced to wear didn't hide her body. She wore a knee-length skirt, and she hadn't hiked it up to catch sight of her legs. On her plate was a slice of pizza and what appeared to be a bunch of fries.

She stepped back, taking deep breaths. Her eyes closed and her lips moved, giving away to the countdown clearly going on inside her head. She hated it here as much as we did, but that was fine.

I picked up a fry and popped it into my mouth, wondering what it would be like to have her squirming on my lap. No one knew anything about Emily. She didn't mingle with any crowds.

We knew who her father was, which wasn't a whole lot of information. No guy sniffed around her.

"He's starting to piss me off," Caleb said.

"He needs to be controlled," this came from River.

Gael snorted. "Please, all he's doing is trying to show daddy he's got a big cock. It doesn't take a genius to know he's got parental issues a mile long. He's much more suited to the prissy school. He'd fit in much better. Let's face it, most of his kind are often sent into obscurity."

"Look at you, using all your big words," I said.

"You fucking the English professor?"

Caleb snorted. "I doubt it. I believe his ass is getting used in a couple of weeks."

We all knew what happened when Mr. Bucati went to Caleb's father. It was all a play to keep him in his place.

Bucati thought he was better than all of us, and it was up to Caleb's daddy to put him in his place.

Shaking my head, I glanced back to see Emily had taken a seat near the doors. She always had her back to the wall. To anyone who hadn't been watching her for the past couple of years, people would assume she was oblivious to the world around her.

Emily was always tense.

She was ready to fight if needed. It was what constantly drew me. There was a darkness within her that she kept in check. I wanted to tease it out, to find the woman she kept trapped inside.

We all had monsters lurking beneath the surface. The difference between us and everyone else was we embraced it.

What was Emily hiding? Why didn't she want to come out and play?

"I think it's your turn to use your knife," Gael said.

"We're still talking about the temperamental bastard?" I looked over to see not one, but four security guys restraining him.

This was what separated Drake from us. The guards wouldn't be allowed anywhere near us. They'd try to intimidate, but they knew who our daddies were, and pushing us would get them fired or dead. I didn't actually know which one would be the kinder of two evils.

"I'm bored," River said. "You think if I cut him

up, it would be okay?"

"I don't think anyone gives a shit about Drake which is why he's always causing trouble." I was done with this conversation. Getting to my feet, I stepped away from the table and walked away.

It was rare for us to go our separate ways, but it happened. Leaving the cafeteria, I headed down to art class and took my seat in the back. Staring at the blank canvas, which I'd been doing for weeks, I waited for the classroom to fill.

As usual, the teacher was late, but seeing Emily arrive first made me smile. She hated art class. She didn't have the talent for it, but I found out her father fucked the art teacher, and it gave him a reason to screw her at school. Lame, but that was our parents for you. The one thing you'd learn about your parents, at least if they were ours, was that they were so fucking selfish. In this life, you often have to take care of number one.

Emily sat in front of me. She wasn't the kind of person to be carrying a bag. It was always in her locker. The only times I ever saw her with it were when she entered school and left.

She ran her fingers through her long, blonde locks, pulling them back. I watched as she used the hair band from her wrist and began to secure her hair into a messy bun on top. She tilted her head left then right before rolling her shoulders.

Again, this was a little routine she seemed to have down. Smiling to myself, I picked up my pencil, and like every single class before, I drew.

The life I had and the one I was running toward wasn't designed for a normal kid. No one in this school was like other eighteen-year-olds out there in the easy world. This school wasn't designed for civilians or for what I considered normal. Seeing what Drake did was a clear enough sign of just how messed-up this school was, and what was more, people liked it that way a lot more than they let on. This was who we were.

When the teacher entered, the class didn't go silent. I was already drawing, so the woman would leave me alone, but as usual, the first person she went to was Emily.

Another smile graced my lips as I watched her gently place a hand on Emily's shoulder, leaning down.

The complete show of favoritism was clear for all to see. What saved Emily was the fact like all the other times before, she brushed the woman's hand off her shoulder, picked up a piece of charcoal, and got to work on scrubbing some kind of mess.

By the end of class, Emily would have, in some way, ruined the teacher's clean white shirt.

I didn't make it a habit to remember teachers' names. My father once told me to keep people in their place. You have to show how little they mean to you. Names were important. They were what everyone was given at birth. It was who you were. It was what made you you. Personally, I thought it was all a lot of bullshit, but what did I know? All I knew was the teachers kept a wide berth of me, and for that, I never remembered their names.

Like now, the teacher in question had come around to my domain. My mask was firmly in place even though on the inside, I was pissing myself with laughter. She wouldn't come too close.

Silence unnerved a lot of people.

My drawing, like so many others, was of Emily. Of course, no one actually knew that as each of my pieces lacked a head. Just a body. What I'd memorized from seeing her in the hallway, or during physical education.

The only other way for me to get a better feel for her would be to touch her. To see her completely naked, and if the rumors are true, her body would be as decorated as mine often was.

Our fathers beat us to be stronger.

I got that.

To take over from the family, you had to be strong. Something didn't sit well with me, though. Emily had an older brother. She wouldn't be taking over the family line. Her life had probably been mapped out with a husband waiting to claim her. She didn't need to be beaten, but I'd already seen the clear signs she had been.

I swiped a hand down my face in an attempt to clear my thoughts of the rising anger, but it didn't help.

I wanted to kill, and Emily's father was my target.

Chapter Three

River

My parents were fighting again.

This wasn't new news. Nothing but old. They fought over nothing. This latest one, my dad had a nice, young, twentysomething secretary. Let's face it, he was fucking her. I listened to one of the many conversations where my parents talked and my dad was insistent this young woman was highly competent and had made his life easier.

My curiosity had been piqued, so I did no more than introduce myself to her and asked a few random, easy questions.

There was no brain there.

Just a good body, plump lips, and my dad's insatiable desire to fuck. His needs were well-known in the Monsters' Crew. They used him as necessary to gain information from unsuspecting women.

I believed my father loved Mom. In fact, I had no doubt. This brand-new secretary was just a means to an end. She probably worked for the enemy and he was using his position and dick to make himself all comfortable with her.

Either way, I was bored.

Getting to my feet, I walked past the office where she was once again threatening to leave. Wives did leave, for a short time, but then life as a civilian was hard work. Cops, the real ones that couldn't be bought off, would circle like vultures, waiting to swoop down and snap them up.

Our lives were a constant balance between getting caught and being fucked. Most of the time, I liked it. When it came to my parents, if my mother left, it would throw my dad off his game.

See, love.

Odd though it was, he had it bad for my mom.

Business always came first.

Loyalty to a wife was always put on hold if the needs of the crew came first.

I slipped out of the house, breathing in the cool air. The two guards who weren't supposed to be seen by me were already following me. They'd been guarding me for two years now. They weren't very good at it. I often gave them the slip, and they didn't have a clue where to look for me.

Tonight, though, with the threats surrounding us, I didn't mind them tagging along as I made my way to Gael's house.

Caleb's, Gael's, Vadik's, and my house were the biggest four within the neighborhood. The way the streets were set up, we controlled the four corners, and the smaller houses were filled with our subjects. Our houses could be seen for miles and for most, it was nothing more than a reminder about what we could do and the power we held within our grasp. Nothing could get past us. We knew everything.

I didn't bother to knock as I got to Gael's house. Stepping inside, I instantly heard the cries.

The kitchen staff were engrossed in their job of feeding.

Weaving my way through, I held my knife in my grip. A look a lot of people had gotten used to. Being taken at sixteen, tortured, and filled with the knowledge you had a whole lot of enemies you didn't know would do that for you. It happened to me, which pissed me off.

My dad caught the guys who'd slashed me up. The scars still decorated my body, and he'd handed the man to me as a gift with a giant pink bow.

I'd always been fascinated by pink. I didn't know why. It was a color I liked. No one would laugh at me though.

Along with being taken, I'd become a keen marksman with my knife.

I didn't have to get far to find the cause of all the moaning.

Gael sat on the stairs, trying to perfect his trick of running a lighter through his fingers. He didn't like how I was able to do it with a knife. He'd been trying for months, and still no such luck.

Staying out of the way of the beating that was happening, I slid down next to Gael.

"What's going on?"

"Bleeding dude tried to go to the cops. Of course, the cops delivered him here. He had a whole load of documents ready and waiting to send to the feds." Gael winced.

I turned to look.

The file of papers was now being stapled to the bleeding man. Screams filled the air with each plunge down of the stapler. The man's nose was already broken, as were his arm and leg. The beating had been really bad.

Clearly, the bastard deserved it.

"Are we out of here?" I asked.

"Yeah, I've seen enough."

We left Gael's house and made our way over to Caleb, who sat out on the porch, scrolling through his cell phone. Vadik already sat on the porch steps, his cell phone out as well. They both pocketed them as we approached.

"I think it's time we paid Drake a visit," I said, looking at my friends. They were more than friends. As far as I was concerned, we were blood, brothers. One unit. Nothing could come between us.

They were the ones who refused to give up on finding me, and now, they had my loyalty and my love for life. We'd always been like that, but being near to death, it changed you.

I knew I was changed. There was a time I'd been like Gael. Fun-loving. Happy to have a laugh. To do anything that would risk our lives. Street racing, dressing up, and going to illegal gambling games, just to get a kick out of seeing their fear when they realized who they were playing with.

Now, for fun, I liked to watch movies. It probably helped that most nights, I couldn't sleep, not for long. I spent way too much time sitting in my window, looking out at the night sky, waiting for the time to pass.

Occasionally I'd pass out from exhaustion, but it happened so very little. The only chance I really had to sleep peacefully was when I was surrounded by my boys. They knew, of course they did.

It was why we'd have nights of hanging out. I'd sleep, and they would watch over me.

This was what made our pact unique.

"And what exactly are we going to do?" Caleb asked. "Tell him he can't be a petulant dick anymore? I think he already knows the score on that front."

"We can't have him continuing to be a prick," Gael said.

"Today he fucked with the cafeteria staff. How much longer will we stand before he tries to take us out? We need to be clear about it," I said. I hated Drake.

He was an unwanted son. A bastard. We all knew it, and because of that, he had a temperament. It pissed him off that no one wanted him.

Poor baby.

"Let's go," Caleb said, getting to his feet. Vadik didn't say a word. Together, in our pack, we made our way out of Caleb's yard and headed toward the main town. All it took was a simple text to discover where Drake was.

He'd settled for the diner.

I liked the food at the diner, so this worked for me as I hadn't eaten since school.

We arrived, finding Drake calmly sitting there and eating his food. There were a couple of guards outside, clearly waiting to delve into any problems.

Caleb took the lead, as he always did, getting us a booth near to where Drake sat.

Picking up the menu, I decided on some burgers and fries. I didn't want anything else.

The waitress came to take our order. I'd noticed long ago that civilians kept a wide berth, even those who worked for us. I always found it funny how scared a lot of people were of us. They had a right to be. Especially after what I just saw. That was child's play compared to some of the other torture methods I'd witnessed.

I'd seen my father so angry, he'd threatened to saw a guy apart, piece by piece, keeping him alive as he did. He was so pissed off, he actually went through with it. There had been a lot of blood, a doctor, and well, it had been an experience I didn't want to repeat any time soon. There would come a time I'd have to do the same thing, or risk someone thinking I was soft.

I shoved my fingers through my hair and glanced at Drake. He shoved at least a forkful of six fries into his mouth, not closing it as he chewed.

At least we had a little more respect.

"What did you guys think of Lauren then? Do you think it's time to take her out for a test drive?" Gael asked.

"No," we all said in unison.

"Oh, come on. Seriously, are you guys going to

get that fucking pissy about this?"

"She's fucked half the school. If you want to have an infected dick by the end of the day, be my guest," Caleb said. "For me, it's a no."

"And me," Vadik said.

"I'm not interested either. I've heard what some of the guys have said about her."

"Yeah, and it means she will know her place. Don't you want to just have a quick and easy fuck?" Gael asked.

We all stared at him so he got the message. Gael groaned and nodded. "You're right. I can still have my fun, though, right? Without pissing you guys off?"

His fun would consist of him stringing the poor girl along, allowing her to believe she had a chance with him, when the truth was, she didn't stand one. She was nothing to him.

"If you want to waste your time."

"A guy's got to do what a guy's got to do."

"This is fucking ridiculous. There's no way I'm paying for this kind of shit." Drake was having another one of his fits. He sounded like a child, and not for the first time, I had to wonder if he even realized it.

"I'm sorry, sir," the waitress said.

She was supposed to be serving us, not this child.

He shoved her hard, forcing her to the floor.

"You're only good for servicing dick, not bringing me my food." He stood and started at his belt, as if he was going to get the woman to suck him off right here, right now. His level of disrespect pissed me off.

Getting to my feet, I stepped in front of him.

I didn't like Drake. Hated him on sight.

Not because of his parentage. To some, that made him scum, not to me. His attitude pissed me off in a big way. We all got that he was pissed at his parents and despised the world. Hello, look where we all were. None of us liked our life, apart from the Monsters, of course. Many a day went by when I thought about ending his miserable life. It would be so much fun to do it. Just a simple blade across the throat. He'd deserve it. I'd watch him bleed out. There were parts of the neck you could slice and it wouldn't kill a person.

"Leave her alone," I said.

Drake smirked.

Gael, Caleb, and Vadik were at my back. The girl scurried away. She was too young and didn't deserve to deal with him.

With my blade in my hand, the threat was there. Drake laughed. "Seriously, you want to threaten me? Do you really have the guts?"

"You're stupid, as well as a fucking moron." I placed the blade against his neck, right near his pulse. "Do you have any idea how long I've waited to do this to you? Every single day of high school, you do something that makes me want to end you."

"My dad…" Perspiration dotted his brow. His face turned a delightful shade of red.

"Let's face it, Drake, your dad wouldn't care. I'd probably get a reward for doing him a favor. You're a piece of shit, and what's more, everyone knows it, yourself included." I pressed just a little harder, seeing a pearl of blood leak out of the tip.

So pretty. Blood turned monsters into men. Into plain old mortals. They didn't have a higher power. I knew how fragile our lives were. The right cut of a blade, the correct mark of a bullet. All of us would be dead. There was no doubt about it in my mind.

We were fragile.

"You continue to fuck around like this, make a scene, ruin the chances of us finishing high school, then I will make you dig your own grave and push you right inside." I withdrew my blade and slapped his face. "Think about that."

****

Gael

"We should have killed him. It would have been more fun," I said.

"And it would have caused trouble for our dads. Just because Drake is unwanted doesn't mean he doesn't have the ability to piss us off," Caleb said.

He was right, I knew he was right. River was thirsting for blood and I had to give it to the guy. I had a whole load of respect for him.

I'd seen what those bastards who took him had done to him. The scars were clearly visible, but we never talked about it. River never wanted to. Personally, I wanted to go back two years and have a lot of fun with them myself. That was never going to happen. I did keep thinking of building a time machine, but what did I know about science? The guilt was what I couldn't stand. Out of all of us, River was the nicest. No doubt about it. He was a good guy. All four of us had been trained to kill, to torture. We knew what our paths meant, the journey we were going to have to take to be in our fathers' places. I wanted it badly.

My first kill was at nine years old. She'd been my nanny. She'd snuck into my family's house, pretending to care for me as if she was a mother. I adored her. She kept the charade up for a year when I discovered her intention to kill my parents and then me. What our little nanny hadn't known was there were secret passages in the walls. One led right to her room, and I'd watched her plan. When she wasn't in her room, I snuck in, saw everything. I had a knack for remembering what a room looked like and I always made sure to put it back. It was the fine details. Like a file pointing left, rather than right, but it also being three inches off the table, rather than one.

One night, I'd snuck in, climbed into bed with her, and then stabbed my knife into her neck. I'd done this five times. Afterward, I'd gone to my parents' room, covered in blood, holding the evidence.

From that day on, I'd been trained. My mother had interfered. The nanny's plot to kill had finally proven to her there were no good people in the world, least of all, civilians. They wanted us dead just like everyone else. There was no getting away from the pain we'd caused.

"Yeah, but pissing us off would be so much fun. We'd have a reason to paint this town red. Don't you want that?"

"No, what I want is for us to head home. I got a code red," Caleb said. We'd been hanging out in the football field.

I'd been ruining said field by burning patches of grass, and also opening and tossing condoms all over the grounds.

I had to get my kicks in some way, and pissing off the football team was so much fun. Even though they were like us in every single way, they liked to pretend they were better, and this was my way of reminding them. They'd come to us as they knew it would be me, pissing on their turf, but whatever.

Once, I'd paid someone to water down cow shit and spread it all over the field before a big game. I'd sat in the stands, munching on popcorn, knowing as they slid down to the ground, their faces pressed to the grass, some with their mouths open, they were eating shit. Good times.

"What the ever-loving fuck is a code red?" I asked. I should know. My dad kept trying to tell me the codes. Pulling out my cell phone, I saw the alert.

"It means someone has gotten past our lines. They're in town, and we need to get to protection," River said.

"Oh, yeah."

The last time a code red happened, River was taken. Not on my fucking watch. Anyone who approached me was going down. I'd gladly fuck anyone up.

I loved a good fight. Where River liked to use his knives, I had my fists. Sure, the cracked skin stung like a motherfucking bitch, but it was so much fun pounding on someone's face.

I was cruising for a fight, desperate for it. It was either fight or fuck.

Some of the girls at school didn't appeal to me. I'd take most to my friends to see if they wanted to share. There was one particular blonde who I hadn't even attempted to capture her attention.

The school was deserted and as we rounded the main front, we all came to a stop.

Six men, all wielding baseball bats. They wore leather cuts, which instantly gave the game away. MC assholes. Their kids never went here. If they did, it would be a whole lot more fun.

One of the men turned, and it fucking pissed me off. The leather cuts didn't have their insignia, which meant this was a direct hit, and it also told us clubs had started to pick sides. The truth was they were fucking cowards. They come into our town, arrive at my school, and they don't even have the balls to wear proper attire. Pissed me off! Fucking cowards.

Their kids probably weren't even theirs. Their old

ladies, or whatever the fuck they called them, must have been getting their pleasure elsewhere.

"Whoever is paying you, you need to consider your options," Caleb said.

Always the one trying to make friends. I'd already clenched my hands into fists.

Baseball bats or not, these fuckers were going down. I wasn't going to run home screaming to daddy. I wanted blood.

"Falls, Block, Parson, and Keller. All four of you here."

They knew our names. The hit wasn't on our family. The hit was on us.

Seconds passed. It felt like minutes. Similar to watching a movie. The moment you faced off with evil. That shot paused as the camera moved around, getting a good picture of all the parties and players. For my movie, I'd give a wink and it would show a twinkle in my eye. I wasn't afraid. I'd never known true fear.

I guessed that was what made me a little weird. Where some felt fear or the adrenaline rush, I felt nothing. This was all mechanical.

Main batter came forward charging toward us, and I struck. Pulling away from my boys, I rushed toward him. After drawing my fist back, I slammed it into his gut. I didn't take the time to look at my boys. I knew they could handle themselves.

I had two guys. One of them struck with the bat, and I ducked. It hit my shoulder. The pain was instant, but I blanked it out, focused instead on fucking them all up.

Grabbing the bat, I twisted it in my grip. River thought I was trying to get it right with a lighter because he could do this shit with a knife, but he was completely mistaken. I did this because it was fun and it saved me time in the long run. This was so much fun.

With the handle in my grip, I drew it back and slammed it against the guy's face. Another slow point that would make for a lot of fun. Laughing, I pulled back, ready to strike again, and moved the bat to connect between the little prick's legs. Down they went.

I checked the time but I didn't know how longit'd been since the fight began. None of the men were dead, but they were on the ground.

I smiled. This was so much fun. This was what I love about fighting. The feeling of power coursing through my veins. Caleb chuckled. Vadik slapped his hands together as if getting rid of dirt.

They all turn to me and that was when I felt the cold muzzle of a gun against the side of my head.

"You little shit. Did no one teach you to never turn your back on your enemy? You're nothing but weak."

I was fucked.

Death was coming to me. The gun was loaded. I knew that. His finger was on the trigger. I looked at my buddies. I wasn't going to cry or piss myself. My father had taught me that death was inevitable. I had to make peace with the fact I was going to die one day.

That day was going to be today.

Staring at them, I knew I'd miss them all. They were my family, my blood, my brothers. Each of them held a piece of my heart. I would gladly die for them. My life would give them chance to get away or attack. Either way, it was a cause I was happy to wait for.

I kept my eyes open. There was no way I was going to allow them to witness my final moments as weak. I was strong.

I was a Monster.

Only, the bullet didn't come.

The man at my side started to choke. The tip of a blade appeared out of his neck. Blood pooled out of his mouth. The grip he had on the gun weakened. The blade disappeared. The man fell to the ground, and the woman behind him was none other than Emily Crane.

She dropped the knife to the ground and it fell with a clatter. There was no shock on her face.

Acceptance.

I watched her as she looked up.

The bag she protected in her locker was on her shoulders, but I saw the mussed-up school uniform and the hair. She appeared to be thoroughly fucked, but I knew when there was no one to pick her up, she hung out at the library. I don't know why she didn't just walk home. I'd stumbled into her many times. Sometimes she'd be studying, other times, she'd be fast asleep. It was those times with her asleep I'd allow myself a few minutes of luxury, watching her.

Silence fell around us.

Emily looked at all four of us and then jerked at the blast of a car horn.

Without a word, she stepped over the body and ran toward said car, leaving us to deal with the mess. Not that it was her mess.

Caleb, River, Vadik, and I all watched her. So many people wanted us dead. Would be happy to see us all six feet under, and against all odds, Emily had saved me. She'd saved the Monsters' Crew. My death would have caused a huge wave of problems, not to mention pain.

She'd fucking saved me.

Why?

Staring at my brothers, I could tell they were all curious as well. Emily didn't mingle with anyone. She didn't pick sides. She was a loner to everyone here.

"We need to get these packed up," Caleb said.

"Dad's going to want to know what happened," River said.

"The knife is here. You say you killed him with it," Vadik said.

I picked up the knife. It wasn't a fancy one like River carried. This was a plain blade. It belonged to Emily. What I'd like to know was how she managed to get past security with this blade. Most of us had weapons on us, but it took a certain amount of bribing to get through the front gates.

I'd always been curious about Emily. She kept to herself. Never interacted with anyone unless she had to. She never had a boyfriend and her life outside of school was a mystery.

Her life had just become my number one priority to figure out.

Chapter Four

Emily

Saving someone shouldn't be considered a fuck-up, but that was exactly what I had done. My dad had texted me earlier that day to say my driver wouldn't be available to pick me up and that I'd have to wait until after five.

The library was my one place of solace. I went there for peace and quiet. Rarely I got the chance to just be, to enjoy my thoughts, to study. I'd fallen asleep and saw that my driver was going to pick me up. If I was late, my driver liked to inform my dad. It would then result in the third degree, where I was likely to get nice new bruises.

I had to remain pure. My dad demanded it of me.

No boyfriends. No lovers. No flirting. There wasn't a single guy at the school he wanted me near. He'd told me the Monsters' Crew were out of my league. There was no way I'd snag a man like that.

My only value was that piece of hymen between my legs. You had to love parents. I felt the love. It didn't stop him from hurting me though. There were even occasions he'd make the doctor come and examine me. That had to be the most humiliating thing of all. The driver hated me. I knew that, for no good reason, but he still hated me. I think he had a thing about women, and he wanted me to suffer the only way he knew how, fucking coward. I hated assholes.

I wasn't late last night, so no interrogation. My dad was in a good mood because of something my brother did, again, so good news for me. So long as they were happy, I was left alone.

Now, arriving at school, I ignored my driver,

climbed out of the car, and made my way into school. No one stopped for me or came toward me.

I had no friends.

I turned down a corridor and came to a stop.

There was no one around but four men, all of who were watching out for me. Gritting my teeth, I squared my shoulders and made my way toward the group. Gael was leaning against my locker.

Holding on to my bag, I stepped toward them, keeping a foot away from them.

I waited.

The silence stretched on.

Usually, the corridor was busy. They had cleared it for this reason.

"Move," I said.

Gael chuckled. "You knew we were going to come for you, Crane."

"What I know is the bell is going to be ringing soon and I've got class to get to. Move out of my way."

"You know, we've hurt people for speaking to us with a little more respect."

"Then kill me, I honestly don't care, but get out of my way." I wasn't afraid of them, nor of death.

Caleb tilted his head to the side, watching me. I hated it, but I didn't avert my gaze. To do so would show weakness. I wasn't weak.

The bruises across my stomach would say it was a lie, but it wasn't. I took each punch from my father. It no longer hurt, and it hadn't been for some time now.

It was why death was so fascinating.

Death would be easy. Like the man I killed last night. The knife I kept in my bag was for protection. I'd never had to use it until last night.

I'd come around the corner, but because I was used to sneaking around, no one had seen or heard me.

The man with the gun had looked so cocky. His stance, the triumph I'd seen just in the side of his face and body language had reminded me of my father.

All of us deserved to die.

I was a fool. I knew we were all going to die soon. I'd welcome it.

That man, though, I was done allowing someone like that to win. So, taking out my knife, I'd done what I needed to do. Killing him had been a pleasure I hadn't anticipated. Only, it hadn't been some biker I'd killed, it had been my father. I wanted to kill him.

"Last night," Gael said.

"I won't tell anyone and seeing as the path is so very clean, I'm guessing you didn't either. Your secret is safe with me." I reached out to my locker. "Now move."

"Why?" Gael asked.

"Did you want me to let him kill you?"

"It wasn't your fight."

"Next time, I'll let them have you. When you save someone, the correct response is thank you. Clearly, no one taught you manners."

River started to chuckle. "And obviously it's the same with you."

"What do you guys want? Do you want some big explanation? You're not going to get it. I saw what was happening, and I reacted. Simple as that. Now can I please get my bag?" I asked nicely.

No one moved. This was a standoff I didn't want to be part of. It sucked.

Putting my hands to my waist, I had no choice but to wait. "You can't keep everyone locked out of here. They're going to need to come into school, and class is going to begin."

The truth was, I didn't want to analyze why I'd done what I did. I'd reacted, that was all it was, and now they were treating me like I'd done something special, when I hadn't.

"You know a lot of people in your position would have killed us," Caleb said.

"I guess I'm not like a lot of people."

Again, all four sets of eyes watched me. I hated feeling like a bug, but there was no way I intended to back down. They were in the wrong here, not me.

In my head, I counted.

If I were to react and my father found out, damn, I'd be fucked. There was no way I'd get away with insulting the entirety of the Monsters' Crew and live to see another day.

I'd take a chance, though, especially daring with my new fascination of the moment, death.

Caleb chuckled. "I can see this isn't getting us anywhere." He turned and I watched as he moved the dial on my locker, opening it up.

"You know my code?"

"I know a lot about everything, Crane. See you around."

Just like that, all four of them sauntered off like they owned the place. They did, but for once, couldn't they at least show a little humility? No, not these guys. They wanted everyone to know who they were and what they did.

I put my bag into my locker, extracted my books, and went about my day.

Math was the first class today, and nothing exciting really happened. This was one of those classes that were filled with the lame kids, myself included. They were the second or third sons, along with the daughters. In reality, I was probably the most important within my class purely because I was Crane's only daughter.

To most, we girls were useless unless we had good looks and a particularly wealthy man wanted to buy us. It would always be disguised as marriage but that was the harsh truth. We were nothing more than cattle to be sold.

I was pretty. My blonde hair always caught attention, as did my lips and eyes. I knew because I'd been told that by many of my father's associates. His biggest issue with me was my curves.

Yep. My dad liked his women super-thin, so he believed every single man did. The only problem was no matter what diet he put me on, or how he starved me, my curves were here to stay. Big ass, rounded stomach and hips, and large tits. My mother said I was blessed with a beautiful body.

One day, I'd find out. If my prospective husband didn't kill me first, that was. I didn't know if my father had a man lined up for me, but I assumed he already did. Most men did. All the girls here were taken in some way.

Like Nancy. With her fancy ring. She was above all of this, but her future husband was in his late twenties, and the rumor about him wasn't very nice. They called him the Butcher. Outside of the Monsters, there were men who could rival them in dirty deeds. Nancy's prospective was that kind of man.

I shook off the doomed feeling. Every now and then, it struck me hard. There were times I'd have a panic attack. When it got so bad at home, my dad would strike me across the face to get me to stop.

Now, I learned to contain myself until I got to the privacy of my bedroom where there was a nice pile of brown paper bags.

After math, it was English.

The one thing to learn at Crude Hill High was to never, ever look down. Always keep your head up, waiting for the next strike. A bowed head was a sign of weakness. School was nothing more than an ocean full of sharks, waiting to dine on their next meal. Bowed head equaled seal, a nice big juicy meal.

Entering English, I took my seat against the window at the back. No one had entered, but Mr. Bucati was there.

We had the old chalkboards, and he wrote some line, probably from Shakespeare. Pushing my legs out in front of me, I lifted my arms and stretched.

The tension within me wasn't going to be doing me any favors.

I nearly jumped out of my seat as Caleb sat down.

No invitation.

No nothing.

Just sat down as if he owned the place.

"What the hell are you doing?" I asked.

"Simple, I'm sitting, getting ready for English." He had this smirk that pissed me off.

"No, not happening. You never sit here. You always sit in the back."

Caleb turned his seat toward me, legs spread, and he leaned back. "Nah, this feels like it's my seat." His smile appeared to be full of promise as he looked over my body.

No one at school had checked me out, at least I hadn't known if they did.

"This isn't funny. You want me to report what happened last night? Is that it?"

"I'm surprised you didn't. You know, for saving Gael, you'd have been rewarded."

I snorted. "I don't want or need any praise. Leave me alone. You've got a full posse of people waiting for you."

There, that was supposed to be the end of it, but I

should have known better. Caleb wasn't about to take no for an answer.

When I grabbed my books, intending to get up, Caleb reached out, putting his large, bear-like paw on my thigh. "Don't even think about it."

"Seriously?"

"I am being deadly serious. By saving one of us last night, you've gained our attention, and believe me, Emily, we're not going to be getting bored anytime soon."

"I don't want this. I want to be left alone."

He smiled and leaned in close. The scent of him reminded me of the earth, fresh, like walking through a forest.

Crazy. So fucking crazy.

"Then you should have let that trigger get pulled."

He was so close, almost within kissing distance, but I didn't want to feel his lips on me. All I wanted to do was be left alone.

If my father found out about this, I honestly didn't know what he'd do.

As I gritted my teeth, Mr. Bucati cleared his throat.

Great, just fucking great.

Hands clenched into fists, I waited, aware throughout the whole class that Caleb watched me.

What fun.

****

Caleb

Emily smelled like lemons. Super sweet and citrus but with a very tart edge. My cock hardened as I stared at her.

She was incredibly beautiful.

Her long, blonde locks cascaded down her back in ringlets. They were natural, I could tell. She also wore barely any makeup.

Everything about her screamed natural and I bet that really pissed her dad off. After what happened last night, all four of our fathers had demanded an explanation for what happened. Emily's involvement had been kept secret.

Until we all knew why she did it, we were keeping her safe. Part of me expected her to want this attention.

The moment she caught sight of us at her locker, though, she'd been pissed. I truly believe what she said when she told us she wished she'd let Gael get it.

Don't get me wrong, the son of a bitch had it coming for turning his back, but Gael was my brother. I had stared at him with that gun pressed against his head. It had only been for a few seconds, but I'd tried to figure out how I could win. How I could protect him, and I came up blank.

He was going to die.

Until I saw that blade appear out of that man's throat.

Emily sneaked around. I got that. She didn't want any kind of attention, and I understood that as well. But, and this was a big but, I wanted to know her. She'd been catching my attention for years, but I'd never approached her. None of us had.

Leaving English, I watched the curves of her ass while she walked away. I wanted to fuck her, no doubt about it. She was all curves and mouth. A temptress, but beneath it all was something dark. She'd killed for us.

Not many girls or women would have done that. They'd have screamed. Probably distracted the guy and got killed. Emily hadn't reacted like a scared woman.

She'd reacted like a fighter, and to me, that made her really important.

I had one more class before lunch. I was starving. Entering biology science, I found River already seated with a knife in hand, pressing the blade against the wooden desks. They were well-used, heavily graffitied.

Taking a seat beside him, I stared up to the front. Our biology teacher was a woman, and she hadn't appeared yet. She was an older woman, late-forties, a bit of a cougar by all accounts. The guys loved her, and I could understand why. Free pussy was always so readily available and with teacher, it meant good grades without even trying.

Mrs. Henchman.

I shook my head.

"Did she say anything?" River asked.

I look toward him.

"Emily."

"I know who you're talking about and no, she didn't say anything." The entirety of English, she sat there and pretended I didn't exist, which I totally loved. I wasn't about to tell him that.

She was a fighter. We needed one of those as well.

"What are we going to do?" he asked.

"Whatever we have to. She hasn't told anyone."

"Why do you think that is? I don't get it. I really fucking don't." He shook his head.

"River, relax."

"You can't tell me that you're not the least bit curious?"

I smiled. "Of course, I am. But I've got a feeling all she wants to do is get through high school without dying."

It was what most eighteen-year-old kids tried to

do. Admittedly, we weren't like most kids.

Mrs. Henchman started the class. A few buttons of her blouse were open, and a couple of the guys in front were basking in the attention.

"You know she's a virgin," River said.

There was no way he was talking about Henchman. It was all about Emily.

"How do you figure?"

"No boyfriend. No husband. No one knows what her dad has planned for her." River's jaw clenched.

This was a sore spot for River. His younger sister, Amelia, had already been sold. Engaged to be married to a man ten years her senior. This was the way it worked in our worlds.

"We should have told our dads," he said.

"And do what? You think they're just going to accept that a Crane daughter stopped one of us getting killed?"

"At least we would have been able to get her in one place. Interrogate her," River said. "School isn't exactly the place."

"You want a chance to be alone with Emily?"

"Yeah. Don't you think we have a right to know?" River looked toward me.

"How about you tell me exactly what I just said, Mr. Falls?" Mrs. Henchman said.

It wasn't unusual to be called upon in class to repeat what a teacher said. I wasn't paying attention. I couldn't give a flying fuck what she was teaching.

I turn toward her. They always tried to humiliate one or more of us. It was their way of showing to the rest of the school we were human.

"You were reminding everyone of the fact you're the school slut. You spread your legs wider than any of the girls here, and what's more, in the eyes of the law, it's child abuse, if not rape."

The class went silent.

"Is that what you wanted me to repeat?" I asked.

Mrs. Henchman's face was as red as the juiciest strawberry. A couple of months ago, she'd asked me to stay behind after class, and pretty much said if I ever needed a warm, wet, willing pussy, hers would be constantly available to me. There was no way a Monster like myself should go without. This bitch was fucking married and many people may not keep the sanctity of marriage. I did, like right now.

Since I turned her down, she'd been looking for ways to embarrass me. She needed to learn I didn't embarrass easily. This was all on her.

"Back to your books," she said, snapping at everyone.

One day, everyone would learn we had the real power, not anyone else. All four of us had been trained to not take shit, to be leaders, to not back down from a fight.

We were the ones with the power.

Class ended. Mrs. Henchman wanted to see me, but I didn't stick around. There was no way I was going to give her the satisfaction.

I left the classroom first with River right behind me. Rather than head straight to the cafeteria, we waited five minutes, meeting up with Vadik and Gael.

Gael was bouncing on the balls of his feet.

"Well, how did it go?" Gael asked.

River sighed. "What is your deal?"

"You guys didn't see your life flash before your eyes? I know I play with death every single day, but I don't want to die." Gael shook his head, gripping the back of his neck.

"You do realize she didn't have any kind of

agenda. She reacted," Vadik said.

"We all know there had to be a reason," I said. I wanted there to be one. The guys didn't know how I'd been keeping tabs on her. She was the only girl in the entire year who hadn't approached us.

I'd even been asked for my autograph, like I'd give something so precious.

After five minutes, all four of us headed to the cafeteria.

It was already thriving and I saw Emily the instant we entered. She was at the checkout. The woman on the register offered her a smile, which I saw her return.

She grabbed her tray and avoided everyone as she got to the table in the corner. Like always, she sat with her back pressed to the wall.

I had to wonder if the others had watched her before. If they knew how she reacted to everyone and everything. Her gaze stayed on the cafeteria, as she never once lowered her guard. Was it like this at home?

I happened to notice the darkness around her eyes. She looked exhausted.

I turn away to get my food, and one by one, I knew everyone's eyes were on us. We had our table, and it was still bare. No one would dare sit where we did.

We had a new destination in mind.

Silence filled the air.

The only sound was of our boots as we walked across the room.

One after the other, our trays landed on the table, surrounding her.

Her hand clenched.

If she made a scene, it would be all over the school. No one here would dare share a video or even take one. Allowing evidence to leave school grounds was a death sentence.

She looked so fucking angry and cute. I loved watching her.

"This isn't funny," she said.

"I'm not laughing." I grabbed my orange juice, gave it a shake, took the cap off, and drank. I enjoyed the refreshing drink.

Her jaw clenched. She wasn't happy and I liked that. Did we unnerve her? I hoped so.

"You did this on purpose so I couldn't leave."

"And how are you liking it so far?" Gael asked.

"I should have let that son of a bitch kill you." She stabbed her fork into her fries and she shoved them into her mouth. Then she picked up a napkin, wiping the corner of her mouth where ketchup had gathered.

Didn't she realize how fascinating she was?

"But you didn't," Gael said.

"And you want to know why." She laughed. "Wow, I'm suddenly Miss Popular because I didn't allow your brains to blow all across the pavement."

"Why do you have a knife?" River asked.

It was at that moment I saw him holding her blade. She noticed it as well. She dropped her fork and glanced past our shoulders.

"You know it's dangerous to keep your backs to everyone. People here would love the opportunity to take one of you out."

"Apart from you," I said.

"Maybe I killed him for me. You ever thought about that?" She looked at each of us in turn.

I laughed. "No, you didn't."

"Stop being a pain in the ass," she said. "He could have raped me and we all know what that means for me." Her face had gone a nice shade of red. She hated it just as much as we did, but she'd just confirmed what I already knew. She was a virgin.

So sweet and so cute.

But also deadly.

A heady combination.

She wouldn't be the kind of wife who would scream or cry in the bedroom. Emily was a fighter. In our world, raped meant damaged goods. Of course, her father would put up a nice show, but any prospects she had would disappear. Most of the men in our world only wanted a virgin.

"Eat," Vadik said.

"I only have one boss in my life. I don't need another."

"Eat," Gael said.

I smiled and it grew wider as River followed.

"Eat," River said.

They waited for me. I looked at Emily.

"Eat," I said.

All four of us. Our own silent communication. All four of us wanted Emily. She intrigued us and with Vadik being the first to commit, it meant this was a sure deal.

What Emily didn't know was she was going to be ours, all four of ours. She was now under our protection. She would be safe and there would be no reason for her to look over her shoulder.

"I take orders at home. Not at school. Next time there's a gun pointed at your head, I'll make sure they paint the streets red with your blood." She picked up her tray and marched away.

Again, silence rang out as she tipped her food into the trash bin.

She was going to be a challenge, but the excitement rushing through me told me I was so looking forward to it.

Chapter Five

Emily

I hated home more than I hated school.

I wasn't safe in any one place, and because of this, I'd arranged my bedroom to offer me as much protection as possible, not that it would do me any good.

Sitting at my desk pointed toward the doorway, I saw my brother standing there. One hand in his pocket, the other holding a lighter.

I stopped doing my homework and watched him instead. Peter had never hurt me unless our father had ordered him to. No man should allow a female to walk all over them, that was what my father said. You needed to learn young that a woman's place was to be silent and in bed.

"How was school?" he asked.

"Fine."

"Rumor has it that the Monsters were attacked the other day."

"Then you know if it's a rumor, it's true."

"I was doing the math," he said, entering my bedroom. He went to the edge of my bed, sitting down.

There was a time we were the best of friends. Even as he sat down, I remembered all the times he'd make me laugh. A little girl getting tickled by her brother, or playing hide and seek. I was damn good at hiding. I knew how to move around this house without anyone noticing. I was pretty sure I could blend into the walls and hear all of my dad's secrets.

The caring brother I loved was gone. He'd grown up and was now more and more like our dad.

Only right now, he had this caring look on his face, which I hated. I wanted to trust it, but I'd learned long ago not to trust anyone. I was on my own. It was why the new blade in my drawer called to me.

There were so many nights I had thought about ending it. Just putting the tip into my flesh, opening up so the blood could leak out, taking my miserable existence along with it.

"I was doing the dates in my head, and it was the same day that you were late home," he said.

"I wasn't late, Peter. My driver was. I was right on time."

"You were right. You know what I find interesting, along with all the cleanup, the security tape has also gone missing, and we all know how important the Monsters' protection is. It's not the first time they've been attacked, and their dads like to gather as many allies as they can."

I put my pencil down.

Years of training had stopped me from showing how nervous I was. "What are you trying to say?" I asked.

Peter smiled. "You know one of my fondest memories was when you would giggle. It didn't matter how long we'd heard our parents yelling at each other, or we'd seen him slap our mom, I would seek you out. Tickle you or tell you a stupid joke and you'd laugh."

"That was a long time ago."

"I miss it." He dropped his head down, looking like the weight of the world was on his shoulders.

"I need to do my homework," I said.

That girl was gone. She'd died many years ago when the reality of who she was and the prison she lived in became apparent.

"I know something went down that day. I'm not saying anything to Dad, but if it did, then you need to be careful around the Monsters. They're not good people."

"And we are?" I asked. "I seem to recall coming home this evening to another doctor visit, Peter. That doesn't make us good people. We're just as bad as them." There was no way I could ever accept that we were good.

I couldn't believe it when I walked home and there was the doctor, looking irritated once again. These visits were coming more regular as I got closer to graduation. This only confirmed my worst fears. They had found me a husband. One who wanted to make sure I stayed untouched.

I fucking hated it.

"Dad got a call from the driver. He said a boy was paying particular attention to you."

I laughed. "I'm starting to think this is my driver's way of getting his kicks. I don't get it. Why do I get punished and yet every time he's proven wrong, he gets nothing?"

Peter opened and closed his mouth. There was nothing for him to say because I was right, and he was so very fucking wrong.

"That won't happen again."

"Because you're going to side with me over Dad? Please. I wasn't born yesterday." I didn't want him here. "I really need to finish my assignment."

Peter nodded. "One day, I hope you find the chance to giggle again."

I didn't laugh. Any sound of amusement that came from my lips was all fake. Happiness was an emotion I wasn't allowed.

My brother left my bedroom and I wished I could breathe easier, but I couldn't. I got back to my homework, hoping the distraction would be enough to help me through it. The sick feeling was back. The tension mounting.

At some point, I heard the doorbell rang. I'd stopped checking to see who it was long ago. My presence was never required, and if my dad needed or wanted me, I was always marched to where he requested me.

I finished all of my homework and put it back in my bag.

With that done, I walked to my window and looked out over the garden. We had two guards patrolling the grounds, not that it was a mansion like the four main houses that dominated this small town.

This also wasn't the smallest house either.

At the sound of a throat clearing, I turned to see Irene standing there, hands clasped firmly together. My dad punched her in the face three days ago, and still, she had a smile on her lips and was more than happy to serve.

I hated this life.

No, I hated my father. If I was a man, I'd have killed him.

"Dinner is served, Miss Emily."

Tapping my fingers against my thigh, I thought about complaining of a stomachache, but I would be hurt for it. If my dad had sent Irene, it meant this was a demand.

I followed behind her, playing the meek young woman I'd been trained to be. My mother was useless. She was probably in some part of the house, passed out on pills and vodka, her poisons of choice.

My shock came in double time as I arrived at the dining room table. My father glared at me, his gaze staring down at my modest dress. Within his walls, I wasn't allowed a pair of jeans or a shirt. My wardrobe was dresses. A woman was only ever granted those. Even my mom, when she was having one of her blank days, had to look the part.

Speaking of, my mother sat at the dining room table, looking very much involved.

It didn't surprise me, what did were the other eight occupants. Each of the Monsters' Crew and their fathers.

"I'd like you all to meet my daughter, Emily." My father moved toward his left side, pulling out a chair for me to sit.

Now the sickness was in my throat. I didn't give anything away, though. I walked toward him. He helped me into the seat, his hand going to my arm, his nails digging into my flesh, providing me with a warning. I was to play the meek girl, or else I'd suffer. I was going to get a beating just because I wasn't wearing a nice-enough dress.

The Monsters here were like royalty and I had fucked up.

"Is that necessary?" Caleb asked.

I shot my gaze toward him. He pointed at my father's hand on my arm.

"I find that action rather distasteful, Bernard," Mr. Falls said.

"My apologies, Daniel," my father said.

"Mr. Falls, Bernard. You do not have the rank or title to be on first-name terms," Mr. Falls said.

With a quick glance around the table, I could see the amusement on every single person's face.

This wasn't good. I would pay for this.

Still, my dad let go of my arm as if he'd been burned. I wished this was progress, but they would leave soon and I'd be alone to face his wrath.

"Of course."

Mr. Falls, within a matter of seconds, had embarrassed my father and his position.

I wanted to know why they were all here, why now. This wasn't good.

Our staff filled the silence by bringing in the food. It didn't matter what they had made, I wouldn't be able to eat a whole lot of it. I took a deep breath. I had learned how to control myself without drawing attention. The tightening in my stomach made me even more uncomfortable.

"This looks like good food," Mr. Keller, Vadik's dad, said.

"We do have a stunning cook," my dad said.

This was so fucking awkward. I chanced a look at my brother, but he didn't give anything away. Why the hell were the Monsters here? I didn't get it. There was no way I'd look in their direction.

"It is so wonderful to have guests here," my mother said.

"You don't have many?" This came from Vadik's dad.

"Oh, I, you see, I sometimes get sick," my mother said. Her cheeks turned a different color.

"My son tells me you're amazing at school," Gael's father said. "I hope my son doesn't give you any trouble."

I had no idea what universe I'd stepped into.

"I don't know about amazing, but I do try hard," I said, pushing my food around my plate. This wasn't fun, not even slightly fun. There was no mention of me going to college. The chance would be a fine thing.

My mom giggled. "Oh, Emily is such a wonderful girl and student. We never have any trouble from her. I believe she's going to become a fine artist."

At that moment, I put some food into my mouth, only to cough at the stupidity of it.

"You draw?" Vadik's dad asked.

I nodded.

"You must be proud, Bernard," Mr. Falls said.

This was too much. They all knew why my dad wanted me to be in art class. My mom wasn't a fool.

"Vadik's really good. He takes art class with me. I've never seen any of his drawings, but our teacher loves him."

This didn't please my dad, his white knuckles a clear indication.

Mr. Keller gripped his son's shoulder. I didn't know what I expected, but it certainly wasn't pride.

"I'm glad. His mother and I don't know where his talent came from, but he has been approached to do a couple of commissions."

Vadik nodded, seeming to play the part of doting soon.

This was just a little too much for me.

Fortunately, the dinner was finished, leaving just enough time for dessert, not that I'd be able to eat the molten chocolate pudding.

We were not normal.

Our families were neighbors, but I knew the true depth of pain they could all inflict. All it would take was a single bullet and my dad would be dead. A snap of their fingers, and my life could be over.

I couldn't help but wonder if it would be so bad. I'd stop worrying about the next punch.

My dad never apologized. There was no guilt here. My mom once told me it would be good for me so I could get used to it. What kind of real mother told her daughter that? I stopped watching movies because of this. Now, I only read study books. Never giving myself a chance to dream of a life away from this.

I was in this for life. My only out was certain death.

****

Gael

Emily hated us, and I found it the cutest thing.

After the disaster of the dinner and dessert, my dad had been the one to speak up first. They wanted to chat with her father, giving us the perfect opportunity to get Emily alone.

We weren't going to tell our fathers about what happened, but seeing as Emily was rarely alone, we didn't have much choice. Caleb was already working on getting us all transferred into her classes.

Right now, all four of us followed her down the garden path, toward the fountain. The guards had been advised to keep their distance. Even her brother had been warned away.

I didn't like any of the Crane men. Her mother was useless as well. It didn't take a genius to work out her mom was a drunk and addicted to pills.

"What is going on?" Emily asked when we got to the fountain edge. It was small, though. My house had one twice the size with naked nymphs spitting water out of their mouths. This just had a circular pillow with water spilling out of the top. There was still enough water to drown a person in, so there was that.

"Nothing," Caleb said.

"That's not nothing. Not once have you or your parents come here. Do you have any idea what you could be doing right now?" Her gaze went to the house.

I looked back but didn't see anyone spying on us. Just because I couldn't see them didn't mean they didn't exist, and with the way she reacted, I guessed it happened a lot. Her life was so carefully structured.

After we made the decision to tell our fathers in one meeting exactly what happened, they had done the rest.

Emily was engaged to be married, but she wasn't aware of the person. We were. He was a wealthy man in his thirties who had a reputation for liking them young. The contract Bernard Crane had signed was for Emily to stay a virgin and three days after graduation, for nearly ten million, she would belong to this tycoon. Only, the man in question dealt in human flesh. He made his money through selling women, trading them, but to the outside world, he dealt in yachts and real estate.

We all had two sides. The side we really were and the façade.

The truth was fear, greed, sex, and money made the world go around. We were just masters of them all.

Vadik took a step forward, as did Caleb. They grabbed her arms, and River pressed the blade against her neck. I happened to notice it was a dull blade. She wriggled, but I pulled her dress up, exposing the bruises across her stomach and the scars from being whipped one too many times.

We knew.

We all let go and she lunged at me first, slamming her fist against my face. I accepted the first blow, but when she went to kick me in the junk, that was unacceptable. I grabbed her arms, spun her around so her body was against me.

She growled. "I fucking hate you."

"You can hate us all you want, but what if I was to tell you we could stop those beatings right now? Today." It was already happening, but she didn't need to know that.

"I think you're all fucking joking. We all know the truth of what goes on behind closed doors. You leave, and I become his own personal punching bag." She tried to wriggle out of my arms.

Each move brought her ass close to my cock, and I had to say, I really did like the feel of her surrounding me. So fucking hot and sweet all at the same time. She made me ache for her. I hadn't even gotten her naked and I knew I wanted her skin to skin. To feel those big tits of hers rubbing across my chest as I fucked her. Her hips would be more than a generous handful.

"Let her go," Caleb said.

"I'm having so much fun." I grunted as pain shot through my foot where she stomped on it.

I let her go and she stood in the circle, facing us. "Look, I don't know what any of this is, okay? I don't need your help and I don't want it." She ran her fingers through her hair, looking up at the house. "I don't want my father to know what happened. He'll be pissed because I didn't say anything."

"And we all know he'll be upset that he couldn't exploit that tiny little detail to get in with our fathers," River said.

"Which brings us back to why you didn't say anything or why you helped," Vadik said.

This time, I remained silent. There was nothing for me to add.

She growled out her frustration. "Can't you guys just accept that I'm nice?"

"We can accept it," I said.

"But anyone else would have worked this in their corner," Caleb said.

Emily laughed, but it wasn't a natural sound. It was forced. She wasn't the least bit happy. Couldn't say I didn't blame her. We were a force to be reckoned with. If we'd gotten the call from her father, none of us would have been interested. She'd be another girl in a long line of those trying to get ahead in this world.

She hadn't acted like other women.

She'd saved me and hadn't exploited my weak position. My father was already aware of the mistake I made and had arranged practice for me to learn from it. That, for me, meant I was going to get the shit kicked out of me until I learned not to turn my back on the enemy. Not bad, all things considered. He could have stabbed me and refused the doctor until he felt I was on death's door, then tried to save me.

My father loved me. All of our fathers loved us. We were the heirs to the thrones. The ones who would take over and keep this place our kingdom. Weakness wouldn't be accepted. At this point, I was the weakest link.

"Wow, so because I didn't want my dad to use this as some kind of negotiation strategy, you're here to make my life hell?"

"Not to make it hell. To make it better," River said, smiling.

"You really don't know what it's like to be a girl in this day and age, do you? To be female in this world." She stared down at her clothes. "Look at the way I'm dressed. You think this is how I want to look?"

She held on to her hair. "That I want my hair this long? Or how about my shoes?" She pointed her toe out. They were heeled shoes, designed to emphasize the woman's calf. "I can't have a boyfriend and don't even get me started on my driver."

The thing about being a Monster and the biggest shark in the sea was that we had a whole lot of spies in our corner. Loyalty meant a great deal to us, and there were many staff members willing to spill every single little detail of what went on inside each of the homes beneath us.

We were aware, as of today, of the random virgin tests she had to undergo.

"I don't need or want you to make this better for me. Just accept what I did and move on. That's all I ask." She pushed past us and I watched her walk away.

After a couple of feet, she tripped but caught herself before she fell. She bent down, removed her shoes, and carried them the rest of the way back into her home.

"I had no idea her life was like this," River said.

I couldn't help but laugh. They all turned toward me as if I was crazy or something. They weren't wrong.

"Come on, you guys seriously didn't think her life sucked? Like mega-sucked?" I shook my head. "She's right. None of us are chicks and the ones we do really know are the kind that don't have to wait around."

"It explains a lot," Vadik said.

"Her dad's a dick," Caleb said. "I don't like him and what's more, I don't think he's on our side. The deal he had going down for Emily, that kind of transfer of cash, it needed to go through one of our fathers, and it didn't. You all saw the way they looked when they discovered that detail. If Crane becomes a traitor, the entire family pays the price of his sins." Caleb folded his arms across his chest.

I didn't like doing our business here, but until our dads were done, we were staying here. We had started this, and now we were going to have to see it through.

"I want her," I said, sliding my hands into my back pockets of my jeans. I was going to buy Emily a pair of jeans just to see a smile on her lips.

She never smiled. I realized that now.

"Listen up, shitface, we all want her," River said. "That was the point of our declaration earlier."

"She's not going to come willingly," Caleb said. "And if our dads agree to the marriage, she's not ours to have."

"No, but she's ours to take and no one will back down once we take her. You heard the terms, Caleb. So long as she remains a virgin."

"You want to fuck the good right out of her?" I asked.

All gazes turned toward me.

I shrugged. "I'm already on board. She saved me when she didn't have to. You've got me down with this chick. I'm intrigued by her. It'll be good to finish senior year with a blast."

Before we had a chance to speak anymore, my dad came out, giving us the signal it was time to leave.

Heading back into the house, I saw Bernard Crane's hands clench into fists, and his jaw tense, as he almost shook with rage. If he so much as laid a hand on Emily, I'd be the one coming for him. Her mother's eyes were glazed and she held a glass of wine in her hand. She wouldn't remember any of this.

After leaving the house, I climbed into my dad's car.

"I want you to be careful, Gael," he said.

"Emily isn't a danger."

"No, she's not, but I don't trust Bernard. I'm going to talk to the others. I don't like this deal he has going on the side. I've already initiated an investigation into the kinds of deals Crane's got going."

"She saved my life, Dad," I said.

"I'm not proud of that, son. I taught you better than that. If she hadn't been there, or if she'd been a real threat, you'd be dead. I have no one to replace you. Do not make that mistake again, do you understand me?"

"Yes."

We drove away from the house. The main driveway wasn't big enough for all of our cars. It was rare for us to drive with our parents. In case anything went bad, we all normally drove separately.

Tonight was a strength in numbers, but I also knew it was a necessity. They had a loose cannon on their hands, and it was time to reel him in.

Glancing in the mirror, I looked back at the house. I spotted a curtain twitch, but I caught sight of her. Our woman was intrigued by us.

Didn't she know that when we put our minds to something, we always get what we wanted? Right at the top of the menu was her.

I couldn't wait for her to cave, for her to belong to us in every single way that mattered. My dick was already hard in anticipation.

Tonight had set about the groundwork. Now I just had to wait, and one day soon, I was going to get her alone.

By the time graduation came, she wasn't going to be a virgin anymore.

Chapter Six

Emily

Tears filled my eyes as the pain from his grip intensified.

"I can't hurt you. They've got you under their protection. You must think you're so smart."

Years of practice told me to keep my mouth shut, so I did. Staring into my father's murderous eyes, I knew he wanted to kill me. To wrap his fingers around my neck and to squeeze the oxygen right out of me. What he didn't seem to get was I wanted him to.

How fucked up was that?

If he killed me now, his life would be forfeit. Someone would know what he did, and he'd be the one running scared.

Instead, I stared right back at him, defying him. I'd always done this. Even as tears leaked from my eyes, the clear indication that my pain was at an almost intolerable level.

I counted in my head, wanting this to be over.

I'd begged before. He'd laughed at me, hurt me some more, and told me for every time I begged, he'd hurt me more. So, I never said a word. I kept my pain to myself.

"Dad," Peter said.

"Fucking slut!" He raised his hand to hit me but the blow never came. "Why the fuck didn't you tell me?"

"Tell you what?"

His fingers were around my throat, cutting off my air supply.

"You fucking bitch!"

He was pulled away by Peter and I gasped for breath, hating that he'd been stopped.

Sitting back up, I stared at my dad. "Just do it," I said. "Fucking kill me. Get it over with." I didn't know where these words were coming from, but the moment they started, I couldn't stop. "I didn't tell you because you didn't have the right to know, and I still wouldn't tell you. You're weak and you would've used it against them. You're not worth it."

He raised his palm, ready to slap me, but I held firm. I wouldn't let him see me flinch, not again.

"You better get the fuck out of my sight," he said.

I got to my feet, but I didn't run as I walked down the hall and went to my room.

I closed the door, flicking the lock into place. It wouldn't save me, but for now, it offered me enough protection to believe I was safe for a short time at least.

After a quick shower and change, I dried my hair as the doorknob jiggled.

"It's me," Peter said.

There was no way I was going to open the door. My dad couldn't hurt me at the Monsters' request, but I was guessing they didn't say anything about my brother. Knowing my dad, he would make sure there was a loophole.

"Are you okay?"

I didn't answer.

"I know you don't trust me, and I'm okay with that. You've been through a lot. I … killing someone, it's not easy."

I took a deep breath. He was wrong. I killed that man and felt nothing. No pain. No anger. I accepted what I'd done, and what was more, I was happy with it. Gael was still alive.

"If you ever need to talk about it, I'd be happy to be the one to help you. I know you're a fighter, Emily."

It sounded like he put his hand to the door, but I

wasn't stupid. That one action could be the difference between letting him know I was weak or staying strong. I opted for strong.

Hands clenched at my sides, I waited.

Nothing.

I took a deep breath, wanting this to be over.

"Goodnight."

I listened to his footsteps and I collapsed to the bed. This wasn't what I needed today. I touched my neck, feeling where my dad had held on to me, determined to make me pay for what I hadn't really done.

Gael, Caleb, Vadik, and River, they'd been here, in my house. They were offering their protection. Why? I wasn't born yesterday. I knew what it meant to be owned by them. Part of me was already owned by the Monsters, as my dad was a minion. It didn't make any of this easier. In fact, it made it a whole lot harder.

Just as I was about to go to sleep, I heard a faint knock. Lifting up in bed, I looked toward my door, but there was no one there. No sign of someone waiting to hurt me. This was crazy, how I had to react in my own home.

Lying back down, I pulled the blankets up closer around me, desperate for sleep to take me away from this crazy day.

The knock happened again, only this time, more persistent.

I turned toward the window and was shocked to find Vadik outside my window.

I push the blankets off and rushed toward the window. "What the hell are you doing?" I asked, opening it wide enough for him to slide on through.

He didn't answer right away, merely looked at me. I folded my arms and gave him a glare. He shouldn't be in my room, so he really shouldn't be judging my attire, but it appeared that was what he was doing.

"It's not good for you to be here. I want you to leave," I said.

"No, you don't." He turned away from me and looked around my bedroom.

My hands clenched into fists. "Excuse me?"

"If you want me to leave, that's fine. But get this, I'm not leaving, at least, not yet." He chuckled. "I've got to say I love this." He moved toward the door, putting his back against it, and stared at my room. "You do this all the time, keep your guard up?"

I ignored him.

"You don't have to answer. I've seen the way you are. At the cafeteria, in school. You rarely allow anyone the privilege of seeing your back. Is that why you walk so fast?"

"Why the sudden interest in me?" I asked. "You know my dad could come up at any minute."

"I know."

"I want you to leave."

"Not happening." He actually bent down and unlaced his boots.

"What the hell? What is … I don't know what I've done to earn this kind of special treatment, and I don't know if you can tell, I don't want it." I stepped toward him, but he'd already kicked them off. Next, his jacket, and then I was silent as he pulled off his shirt.

I stepped back.

"I'm not going to hurt you."

Shaking my head, all I could think about were those damn doctor appointments. "If my dad finds you here…"

"He won't. Believe me, he's got a lot on his mind."

"I don't know why you're here."

"To hold you, that's all."

This was insane. "You can hold any other girl. Why me? Is it because I don't fall at your feet, is that it? You want me to fold, to be yours? Is it because I saved Gael?"

"You think this has to do with you killing someone or because you're not a slut like some girls?"

"Ugh, don't do that. Don't call girls that. They're no different than you. I hate that." My hands clenched into fists. I found the double standards between men and women so fucking stupid. Like they were perfect. Yeah, right. A woman goes around sleeping with random men, she's a slut, a guy does it, he's a stud.

Vadik held his hands up in the air. "Sorry, my bad."

"I don't find this funny."

"Have you ever allowed yourself the chance to relax?" he asked.

There was no point in answering.

"I'm not going to try anything, but learn to trust me. You've been on your own for too long. I'm going to prove to you we're not all bad."

"Are you kidding me right now? The last guy I trusted turned against me." He was my brother. He was the last person I'd given a shit about and look what happened there.

Vadik didn't say anything. He stepped toward me.

I stayed firmly in place. There was no way I was going to be intimidated by his getting closer. My heart raced. The moment he was in front of me, he cupped my face.

"I think it's time you learned to trust me, to trust us."

"The Monster Boys?"

He smirked. "We're more of a crew, don't you think?"

"I don't think about you."

"Now you're just breaking my heart."

"So there is a heart to break inside your chest?"

"Baby, there is always a heart to break. I'm not a complete monster."

He took hold of my hand, placing it directly over his chest. His heart beat firmly beneath my palm.

"Do you feel that? It means I'm alive. It means you're not alone. You will never be alone. Not while I'm here. I will always come to you."

"You don't even know me." There was no way I could trust this. I wasn't stupid. This had to be some kind of trick.

"But I want to get to know you. Is that so hard for you to believe?"

The truth was *yes*.

For the past few years, I wasn't the kind of person people noticed unless they wanted to hurt. In school, I kept a wide berth of friends. It was easier. In our world, betrayal ran deep. Loyalty was everything and yet so very rarely given.

I nodded my head.

I was tired and no longer wanted to argue. I pulled my hand away from his very firm, muscular chest. Hard not to notice with my hand flat against him.

After climbing into bed, I pulled the blankets up to my shoulders and turned off the light. I heard him moving around. His footfalls were light, though. Seconds later, he climbed in beside me.

My bed was large, but he seemed to make it so much smaller.

I couldn't help but smile, only to freeze up as he curved his body around mine. His pelvis and a very hard cock pressed against my back. I bolted upright, turned my light on, and glared.

"What the hell?"

"You say that a lot."

"I didn't … we're not going to have sex."

"Baby, I told you, you're safe with me, but don't think I'm not going to get turned on. I am."

"Why?"

The smug smirk was back in place as he put a hand on my knee. "Would it be so hard for you to believe it's because you're fucking hot?"

"I don't … huh?"

"Emily, you've got a body that I want naked, beneath me. I'm not going to force you though. You've made it perfectly clear you don't want that, and I'm not into rape."

"But you are into holding me, so Gael can lift my dress?"

"I'm into finding out all the answers to what makes you tick. It's what I'm good at. You won't like it, but the truth is I don't give a flying fuck. I like you. This is me stating that to you."

"Okay, you like me. I don't know what that means because you know I can't … we can't…"

"Not yet, but it's your life."

"Don't sound like an idiot, Vadik, it doesn't suit you. None of this is my life. I don't have a choice. My choices were wiped away the moment my mom gave birth to me in this shithole. You saw her. She's as good as dead inside." I stared down at his hand. He still touched me. "That will be me one day."

"It doesn't have to be."

I hated that tears filled my eyes. I didn't allow them to fall as I gritted my teeth. "You need to learn not to give people false hope. It's not very nice."

With that, I pushed his hand off my thigh, turned off the light, and settled back into bed. Vadik wasn't done.

His arm banded around my waist, and he got himself comfortable right against my back. At first, I was tense, but the truth was, it was the safest I'd felt in a really long time.

****

River

Vadik arrived at our meeting spot near the lake looking too damn happy.

Caleb stared, as did Gael.

"You went back to her place," Caleb said.

"I didn't hear any instructions not to."

"You fuck her?" Gael asked.

The smile on Vadik's face vanished.

Gael held his hands up. "Got to wonder. One minute she can't stand us, the next she's offering you a space in her bed. A guy's got to be curious about the sudden change of heart."

"No, I didn't fuck her."

"But you want to," Caleb said.

"I think it's safe to say we all want a piece of her," I said, speaking up.

School would be starting in half an hour. I didn't want us to be arguing about these little facts for too long.

Caleb stood tall. "So we all want her?"

We all responded with a nod. Me? I didn't completely know the other guys' deal with Emily. I only knew my interest. It wasn't so much interest as curiosity. I didn't know who I was trying to kid. I wanted her, period.

I'd noticed her a few years ago. Her long, blonde hair captured my attention. Then the curves of her ass. I happened to love a nice, juicy ass, and Emily, she had one. It had gotten bigger in the past two years, and her hips as well. Her body was a wet dream.

"It appears that way."

"Is this going to be a problem?" Caleb asked.

"I don't see why it should be," I said. I looked at my best friends, my brothers. "We've shared a woman before. It's not like we don't know how this is going to go. We all want a piece of her, and so long as we learn to be nice, I don't see why this can't work."

"We're talking about sharing a woman. Is this for a short time, or are we really going to do this?" Vadik asked.

"I say we share her," Gael said.

"I don't see why not. All four of us want her, and we know how to share. We've been doing this shit since we were first born. A woman will be easy."

"She's not going to be easy to win over," Vadik said.

"That's not a problem," Caleb said. "We're all very patient men. She's got to know who she is dealing with." He smiled.

"Is this until graduation or after?" I asked. "Because I can see that look on all of your faces. Emily isn't a quick fuck. She's not a piece of weekend fun. We do this, it has to be for life. We know our parents won't agree to this. She will only ever be able to have kids one at a time."

"Unless we are fucking lucky, and she gives us all twins," Gael said. "I'm a glass-half-full kind of guy, and that's not about to change now."

I shook my head. "So let's call this to graduation. None of us make plans until after then."

"What about her proposed?" Vadik asked. "According to my dad, they didn't resolve that issue."

"But they're looking into it," Caleb said. "There's no way they're going to allow this to go ahead, not this year. I doubt it."

"Just because we don't think it will happen doesn't mean it won't," I said. They had to keep their heads on straight, otherwise, they were in for a shock.

Gael pulled his sleeve up. "It's time we got the hell out of here. I don't want to be late for class. I hear it's going to be exciting."

"Do we have any ground rules?" I asked.

They all stopped walking to their respective cars. I drove in with Caleb.

"What do you mean rules?"

"If one of us fucks her? None of us. Can we kiss her? Can we treat her like our own or do we have to wait until each other shows up?" I wanted to make sure we remain friends. They seemed oblivious to the possible repercussions of falling for the same girl. My dad had warned me last night how vital it was for me to keep my head on straight.

"We don't have to be in a group. That's not going to win her over," Caleb said. "And I'm not waiting around for you fuckers. You have a chance with her, you take it. End of."

That was all I needed to hear.

Moving toward the car, I climbed into the passenger side just as Caleb fired up the car.

"What was with all your questions this morning?" Caleb asked.

"I want to make sure I'm clear on all the fine points. Our friendship comes first. It always will."

Caleb sighed. "You think she's a problem? If you don't want her…"

"You don't have a clue right now. Just drive."

"You think you can get away with telling me

what to do?"

"I just did." I smiled as I turn toward him. "And you're doing it."

"Asshole."

I was just having a joke. I rarely did it anymore. Since my kidnapping, I'd become the more serious one of the group. Seeing as Caleb was our leader, that had to say something. I remember pissing him off because I didn't take anything too seriously I'd joke with Gael, constantly pulling pranks. It pissed Caleb and Vadik off all the time.

We were all the best of friends, but that didn't mean either of us had our true soul mate as a friend. Mine used to be Gael.

Now, I didn't know who it was.

Vadik and Caleb were their own little unit at one point. Both of them serious. Both of them ready to take on the world, but then they were older than us by a couple of days.

"You do want her?"

"Caleb, I've wanted her for a lot longer than the past few weeks." I rolled my head to look at him. "I just don't talk about it as she was off-limits."

"She is off-limits. My dad said. Not until he's figured out this deal."

"Let's talk business." I'd rather talk shop than my feelings when it came to Emily. We were the best of friends, but some shit wasn't up for sharing. "Bernard Crane isn't a Monster. He's not even high up in the food chain, yet, if you looked at that house last night."

"He's not hurting for cash," Caleb said. "I did notice that."

"He runs a couple of gambling joints, deals with a few MCs." I stopped.

"You have a feeling he's the one who sent the

bikers?" Caleb asked.

"I have no idea. You think he would?"

"I don't know. Yesterday I'd have said not a chance, but after last night, I've got a feeling there's more to Bernard Crane than we want to know."

I didn't like where my thoughts were going.

"If he turns out to be a traitor, Caleb… You know what this means?"

"Yes."

Emily would be the one to pay the price along with her father, brother, and mother. Even the damn family pets, but it didn't appear as if he owned any dogs or cats.

"What do we do?" I asked.

"We wait. We keep a close eye on Emily, and an even closer one on our dads. We stay by their side. We stay in the loop. No slacking off. We need to give Gael and Vadik the update." Caleb slammed his hand against the steering wheel. "I knew he was a piece of shit. Fucking knew it."

"We don't know the whole story."

"What we do know is the fact he was able to negotiate this deal for some time. He's had this tycoon in his pocket, and until last night, we didn't know shit."

"Unless our dads did know and are keeping us out of the loop." It wouldn't be unheard of. To them, we are just boys, no matter how much earned our ink. They would see us as their babies, and not in a place to go taking theirs.

"I don't want to think about that."

"You're going to have to. You need to realize that a lot of shit goes down for a reason. We're not going to always like it, but it happens. Remember what they told us. They will always come first. Their reputation is what they will fight for." Caleb arrived at school. Drake was at the front gates, leaning against it, smoking.

He'd taken the hint and quieted down. I didn't for a second believe we'd warned him sufficiently. He would be coming back at us, only harder.

Vadik and Gael were already waiting. Whenever we arrived at school, it had to be a united front.

I followed Caleb in.

We never used our lockers. There was no point in it, but we made one stop, Emily's. She stood at the locker. The school-policy skirt rode just above her knees. She always wore hers at the waist and never tried to pull it up. It was always in the same place.

"Hello, beautiful," Gael said.

She tensed up, turning toward us.

"This is how you're going to play this? You're going to be my new BFFs?" she asked. She put her bag into her locker, grabbed her books, and turned toward us.

We'd already gained some attention.

A couple of the girls looked a little shocked that all four of us surrounded Emily.

She'd been a nobody, not just because of her silence within the school grounds, but her father's position as well. He was neither a right-hand nor a left-hand man to our fathers. He was nothing more than a simple minion.

The school and rumor mill would be rife. Gael would probably play to it. Not that I'd blame him.

She needed to know who she belonged to, and we'd waited a little too long to stake our claim.

The thought of an old bastard waiting for her virginity sickened me and pissed me off. Also, there was a great deal of jealousy. I was River Block, one of the four heirs to the Monsters, and I wanted something I couldn't have. This was a brand-new experience for me, and not one I wanted to think about or relish.

I wanted this woman. I was going to have her as well.

It had been a long time since I'd felt this way. This fire. This need, and it was all for Emily.

"You know, we could make you the most popular girl in school."

This made her laugh. "Seriously, you're going with that?" She shook her head and looked around. "In case you didn't get the memo, I don't want to be the most popular girl in school. Do you have any kind of idea what being seen with you four means?"

"You belong to us," I said, putting my hand on the locker.

She looked at my hand. I had scars on my fingers from the training I'd taken with my knife. I didn't have it in my hand right now, but it was in my pocket. I normally held it to help focus my thoughts, to keep me grounded, only, I didn't need it. Staring at Emily, I realized she was all the grounding I needed.

Well, shit.

Emily laughed. "Good one. I don't belong to anyone."

"Until your father sells you?" Caleb asked.

Her face heated and she licked her lips. Damn, that tongue would look so good sliding up and down my dick. One day. She would belong to each of us. We could protect her. No old bastard was going to be taking her from us.

"I have to get to class." She turned on her heel as if to walk away, but Gael stopped her exit. "Please, move."

"Give me a kiss and I'll let you pass."

I watched and waited. She stepped up close to Gael. I'd have given anything to feel those lips on my face, on any part of my body.

She took us all by surprise as she drew her knee up and caught him in the balls. Gael hadn't been expecting the blow and collapsed to the ground, grabbing his junk.

This was going to be so much fun.

Emily would be tamed. I had no doubt about it.

Chapter Seven

Emily

There was a time I used to love gossip. It was so much fun to find out who the latest target was. Especially when I knew it wasn't me. Of course, some of it was complete nonsense. A girl being pregnant or aliens had landed in someone's back yard. Then there were the other kinds of gossip. The truth.

Like the whispered words I heard today of the Monster Boys wanting little old *moi*. Yep. The gossip rumor mill had been swirling all day since I'd been surrounded by all four of them. It didn't help that Gael had puckered up, and even if my virginal lips wanted to kiss him, I hadn't.

They were dangerous. Not that danger was a problem. It was part of my life twenty-four seven.

What hadn't been in my life was their attention and because of them, I didn't know how my father was going to react. There were so many more interesting ways he could make me pay. My dad was a master manipulator and he knew how to make it so he didn't break any rules. He once told me the world was full of loopholes, all you had to do was exploit them. Weakness was something my father constantly looked for. I didn't know how to handle this side of him now. The part where he wasn't the king of his castle.

It was what Caleb, Vadik, Gael, and River had done last night. All four of them, or more importantly their fathers. They'd come into his home and took his control. That had to have consequences, and it was always those who didn't deserve it that took the brunt of the punishment.

I had a feeling he'd use my brother.

Arriving at the changing rooms for physical education, I took my gym clothes and went to the bathroom. After sliding out of my uniform, I changed it for the gym stuff the school demanded we wear.

Once dressed and my hair was tied back, I left the bathroom. Only Nancy remained, tying up her shoelace.

"Hey," she said.

"Hey."

"So, it's turned out to be a crazy year, right?"

I looked at her. We didn't do small talk.

Nibbling on my lip, I kept on staring at her until her face went a nice shade of red.

"I'm sorry. I didn't realize you didn't talk." Nancy let out a little giggle.

"I do talk and you know that. What I want to know is why you're talking to me." I folded my arms across my chest.

"Not everyone is a bad person."

"We go to Crude Hill High. You know what our parents are capable of and what they do behind closed doors. Everyone here is a bad person or related to someone bad. There is no innocence here."

"Why are you being such a bitch?"

"No, I'm being real. You don't want that reality check? The only reason you're talking to me now is because four guys turned up at my locker. I'm sure your cheer group want all the details, if not to offer me a spot on the squad, right?"

Again, the deep red color intensified.

I burst out laughing. "They sent you because they know you're the nicest of them all. I get it, I do. They want all the gory details and the chance to find out how to snag one of them for themselves. You become the wife of one of the Monsters, you have it made, right?"

Nancy stumbled over her words.

"Don't call me a bitch when you were using me and what's more, don't allow yourself to be pushed into a fucking position you don't want." Slamming my locker closed, I was done.

I liked Nancy. She was the nicest of the entire school. Too nice, but it also meant she was easily manipulated, which made her at the bottom of the making-friends list for me. None of the people at this school were worth lowering my guard for.

Arriving out at the track was our gym teacher, Mr. Avery. He held a clipboard in his hand.

I stood at the end and shouted out my attendance when he got to my name.

All four of the Monsters were in my gym class.

This was new. I'd never been to gym with them here before. Shaking that weird feeling, I focused on Mr. Avery. He was one of the few teachers who didn't seem to pretend he was better than anyone else.

The watch he wore was worth more than his salary could afford. He probably had a long list of bribes for turning the other way when dealing with some of his football players.

The football team was good and a few of the players would have made it as professionals. A couple whose families had allowed them to even went on to have amazing football careers. An odd occurrence, but it happened.

Nancy joined us and Avery chewed her ass out for her tardiness. I wasn't happy about it. I didn't like that she was so easily used.

In this school, we had to keep our guard up, to fight our corner when the occasion called for it.

"Hello, beautiful," Gael said, the first to approach.

I ignored him.

A couple of the cheerleading squad held their hands up and talked behind them as if that covered the fact they were gossiping.

There were two ways to play this, ignore or face them.

Ignoring would be easy.

With hands on my hips, I turned toward them, forcing a smile to my lips. I wasn't confident about this. Far from it, in fact.

"Hey, you've never been in this class before. Why are you suddenly here?" I asked.

He reached out, putting a hand on my hip. "What do you know? I got the update this morning. The principal took me into class and told me there had been a change to my schedule. It appears we'll be having gym together for the rest of the year."

"Parson, you can fuck around on your free time. In my class, you run when I say. Everyone to the line." Avery yelled that last part.

Running was something I hated to do. It wasn't fun.

Gripping my shoulders, I stretched out my neck, trying to think of anything that would be a lot more fun than running for no good reason. It wasn't like any of us were going to be able to take this up outside in the real world.

Running was for cowards.

I guessed being a woman, I might get away with it. Running, though, provided a target.

Avery screamed for us all to run as he blew the whistle.

The jocks in my class took off at the speed of light. Before the end of this lesson, they would be throwing up. It was a good thing this was before lunch and not after it. Avery had been my teacher for two years. He was a nice coach. He'd seen a couple of the bruises on my body and had been really sweet. Not inappropriate. He was a happily married man who had no choice but to take this life after his brother dragged him into it over a gambling debt.

He made me wish our kind didn't exist, but like he once told me, the world needs criminals.

For me, it didn't, but the truth was you needed evil to have good.

That was what I saw us all as, evil. I knew my father was responsible for killing innocent people. Their blood was on his hands and while I lived in his house, it was also on mine.

The cheerleaders stayed near me. They were so close I could smell their perfume. The only reason they stayed close, was yep, the Monsters surrounded me. Gael on one side, River the other, Vadik behind, with Caleb a little in the front.

I always paced myself during running. There was no easy way to get through it.

For an hour, we'd have to run our asses off, and I knew there would come a point when it would be a slow walk, but then Avery would yell, and I'd try to run again.

By lunchtime, I'd be starving.

I hoped I'd be able to eat. If I felt sick, it would be impossible for me.

"So, you're now all in my gym class?" I asked.

"You got it, babe."

"Do you guys even go to gym?" I was already out of breath, but they appeared to be in their element. It made me hate them just a little bit more.

My heart raced.

"If you're asking if we can handle this, see for yourself," Caleb said.

He'd turned so he ran backward.

"Are you flirting with me?" The question was out of my mouth before I could stop it.

"You tell me. I must be rusty if you have to ask." Caleb winked at me.

"Are you wearing a sports bra?" Gael asked.

I looked toward him then wish I hadn't as he stared down at my chest.

"How old are you?" I asked. You'd think guys would grow out of mocking a girl for her tits bouncing in senior year. All of that shit should have ended ages ago.

"I'm eighteen, and believe me, I do not have a problem with what I'm seeing."

Now it was my turn to be embarrassed.

I looked away from him and focused on the ground instead.

For ten minutes, I was able to keep it up, but after that, I was sweating buckets. I would have to use the shower, and that meant I'd wait until all the other girls had left, and I'd arrive late at lunch.

Great, just great.

I was starving already, sweaty.

The Monsters weren't helping me at all. There was no way I could enjoy this. Not with them hovering over my shoulder like they owned the place. They did, but that was beside the point.

I couldn't help but think about the blade I had stored back in my drawer at home. With Vadik in my room last night, there was no way for me to use it. I'd have loved to, though. To put the tip to my wrist, to slice it on through so my dad's plans would be forever broken. The last person I wanted to see win was that man. He deserved to suffer and I was more than happy to go along with those plans.

It was all I could think about at this time. To see him suffer.

Would it be possible to ruin his future with the help of the Monsters? Could I use these four guys to do that? What would be so wrong with having sex, kissing, being a teenage girl just once?

My thoughts got the better of me and I tripped over my feet. I would've gone face-first to the ground if it wasn't for Caleb catching me.

"You better be careful. Otherwise, I'm going to have to make a habit of being in front of you all the time."

That smirk. They all had one, it was just a different level of crazy. I pulled myself away from him, brushed down the front of my uniform, and kept on running.

No matter how deadly or dangerous these guys were, I wasn't going to use them for my own personal gain. I wasn't my dad, and I never would be.

****

Vadik

"She's playing hard to get," River said.

We leaned against the wall outside of the changing rooms. Gym had ended ten minutes ago. Most of the girls had left, but there was no sign of Emily. I'd been the one showered and dressed fastest out of the guys, so I would have known if she'd snuck out.

She'd been sweaty so she'd have no choice but to shower.

After another couple of minutes passed with no sign of her, I'd seen enough. Even as Caleb called my name, I stepped into the changing room.

Most of the locker doors were open, but one was still locked, and I'd have to bet it was Emily. The sound of a shower running confirmed it. Even if my boys thought this was a bad idea, they didn't stay outside waiting for me. They followed right behind me.

I was used to making an entrance. We all were, but right now, we were all trying to be silent.

A small hum could be heard over the spray of the water. Coming to a stop at the entrance of the shower, I paused. There, in the corner, stood Emily. She was completely naked, showcasing the curves of her ass and thick thighs. She turned a little. Her eyes were closed, and she tilted her head back, giving us a beautiful view of her body.

I looked my fill. My dick was already hard. Big tits, a rounded stomach with a bruise. Where clothes would cover her, her skin had different shades of bruising. Even her arms above the sleeve line of her shirt had finger marks.

She turned again and that was when I saw the lines across her back. They weren't recent, but it showed she'd been whipped, possibly with a belt. The scars had healed but it had been deep.

I had similar marks due to my training. My father liked to get his men to beat me, to break me down until I was nothing more than an animal, and I was to fight my way out. From what I could gather, my grandfather had done the same to him. I hoped my dad didn't expect me to kill him like he did his father. It would be the full circle, one I refused to repeat. You could make men strong without turning them almost feral to do it.

It was why I didn't like talking so much. Words got people killed. Those marks on her body, I just knew came from her father. I'd hated the bastard on sight but now, seeing this, knowing he was hurting her, well, it pissed me off even more. One day, I was going to kill that fucker, and when I did, it was going to be with a smile on my face.

As I looked at Emily, I knew she was a goddess,

and I believed now more than ever that she was sent down for us. Her body, her attitude, we could tame her, but also nurture her. She'd been hurt a lot in her life, and with us, we'd be able to tame that beast swirling within her.

I'd been so focused on her ass, I hadn't realized the shower turned off or Emily had caught sight of us. She screamed, grabbing a towel.

"What the fuck are you doing here?"

I hadn't heard her talk a whole lot but I love the way *fuck* rolled off her tongue. It was sexy as fuck.

She pressed her towel to her, trying to keep herself covered.

Gael slid right on past me. "We were waiting for you," he said.

"Not here. Not now. Get the hell out. I can't believe you. Spying on me." She stepped away from Gael, but I decided to have some fun and moved toward her other side, keeping her trapped. River followed Caleb, closing the space until we were within touching distance. We could have so much fun with her, and I wanted to. I saw the way her pulse beat rapidly against her neck.

So tender.

So delicate.

Caleb was the first to reach out and cup her cheek.

She backed away. "I'll scream."

"Please do," Gael said.

"So this is what the all mighty Monsters do? They corner a girl in the shower and what? Rape her?"

Caleb laughed. "I don't need to use force to get what I want, but you, Emily, you have certainly been a surprise."

The passion in his voice was clear to hear. We

were all feeling it. All of this was inspired by her. Our woman.

"I don't like this. Please, leave."

Caleb ran his thumb across her lips. "But I don't think you want us to leave. Your mouth speaks shit your body doesn't want."

"What? Every girl wants you so you assume I do as well?"

"Not every girl gets us," Gael said.

"I don't want to play this game."

"The only way you're going to get past us is with a kiss."

"A kiss?" she asked.

"Yes. We'll allow you to leave, but you have to pick one of us to kiss."

It didn't matter who she picked. All it meant was by the time this kiss ended, they'd be at the end of the line until next time.

"A kiss. To allow me to get changed and to go to lunch?" she asked.

"Yes."

"That's it. A kiss?"

"Yes. Do we have a deal?"

She shook Caleb's hand. "Deal." She turned toward me and placed a kiss on the tip of my nose, shocking me. "You never specified how I was to kiss. Will you break your word?"

Caleb chuckled and moved out of the way.

Even with the towel, it wasn't much for modesty.

My nose fucking tingled from that kiss.

We followed her out toward the lockers and she turned with a glare.

"Seriously, can I have some privacy?"

"The bruises," River said. "Your dad has been following our instructions?"

She snorted. "Yes, of course, and if I know my dad, he'll be figuring out ways to make sure you don't do shit about it." She tightened the towel around her body before reaching into her locker, pulling panties on, and sliding them up her thighs.

I wanted to spread them wide, to lick at her pussy, to taste her and hear her screams as she came against my tongue. Instead, I had to watch item by item be pulled on. When it came to the bra, she managed to clip it on over her towel, slide the towel out, and secure those tits away from my sight.

Damn.

Next, she buttoned up her shirt.

"You have no idea who you're dealing with," she said.

Caleb laughed and I followed suit.

"No, Emily, you need to realize you have no idea who *you're* dealing with. Next time, that kiss you think you've won will occur on your pussy and you'll be riding one of our faces while the others watch." Caleb invaded her space, took her face in his hands, and slammed his lips down on hers.

She tried to pull back, but Caleb didn't let her go. He punished her by making her ache for him.

I smiled as I watched her hands go from clenched fists to softened grips on Caleb's arms. She wasn't as elusive as she made out to be.

The sound of her stomach rumbling filled the silence.

"It's time to get you to eat."

River closed her locker while Gael picked up her bag.

"You guys aren't going to stop this, are you?" she asked.

"Nope. We're by your side for the considerable

93

future."

She sighed. "If I'd let Gael die, would you have left me alone?"

This had us all pausing.

Caleb, like always, took the lead. "I guess we're never going to know the answer to that." He winked at her.

We could be like this, playful, teasing. But there was another side to us that I hoped she never got to see anytime soon.

I followed close behind as we walked into the cafeteria, Gael still carrying her bag. Caleb and I went to our table, leading Emily right beside us.

Silence met our entrance and continued as we sat together.

"What are you guys fucking staring at?" Gael asked. He'd jumped the line and had two trays loaded with food.

Everyone instantly started to look elsewhere. Gael put the trays on the table with a clatter and gave a once-over to make sure no one stared. River joined us a couple of seconds later, laughing.

"I'm guessing this is the best thing since the latest reality show," River said.

I grabbed the fries with the chili on. I had a thing for spice. I craved it nearly every single day.

After I pushed my plate a little toward Emily, she took what I offered, closing her eyes as she chewed. "Yum."

Caleb put the burger in front of her. River went for the salad with beef. I stayed with my chili fries.

"What are you doing tonight?" Gael asked.

"Let's see, it's like every night. I'll get picked up, go home, and do homework." She didn't say anything else.

I was curious about the doctor visits. I wanted to know more.

"Not tonight," Gael said. He pulled out his cell phone and typed on it. "Already arranged. My dad is handling it."

"You can't do this," she said.

"Do what? Give you a life that's a little more exciting than going home to your dad and doing homework? You do know you're not going to college, right?" Gael asked.

She shook her head. "There's nothing wrong with getting perfect grades."

"And there's nothing wrong with having some fun. We're going to show you how to party."

We started eating again, but I saw Emily's hands clenched together. Her knuckles white.

"What happens after?" she asked. "What happens when you have your fun? You dump me on the ground like you did Lauren, what then?"

"Not going to happen," Gael said. "You're different and you know that."

"All I know is you guys are used to getting your own way. You leave a trail of crap in your wake and don't think about the people you screw over while you do." She got to her feet and without another backward glance, left the cafeteria.

Picking up a fry, I got to my feet. Art class was the one place I'd have her all to myself. My boys could do a lot of things, but drawing wasn't one of them. They were a lot like Emily.

I held my hand out for the backpack. "See you in an hour," I said.

Walking out of the cafeteria, I left it to the guys to get shit in order. We didn't need people thinking they could start stepping all over us.

The art room was the only place Emily would go. When I arrived, I found her slumped outside of the room, her head in her hands.

"You're not going inside?" I asked.

"I'd rather stay out here."

Stepping over her, I checked through the glass and sure enough, her father had the art teacher naked and was fucking her like a mad dog.

"Wow," I said. "I thought he waited 'til parent-teacher night."

"Clearly he's pissed with everything going on."

I slid down the wall, sitting beside her.

"What's it like to be able to do everything you want?" she asked. "Without someone waiting to hurt you?"

I laughed. "I'm sorry. You think we don't suffer? You think it's easy for us?"

"You walk around school like you own the place. You don't ever have to worry. Your lives are your own."

"No, they're not. We don't have to stick to the strict rules like you do. We're different there, but that doesn't mean our lives are easy. They're not. It's fucked up in a big way. We could be forced into an arranged marriage." I doubted my dad would do it. If you had to stay with a nag, you may as well stay with one you loved, or at least cared about.

Something bound our fathers together. I wasn't an idiot, I knew friendship went a whole lot deeper for our dads. It kept them loyal to one another. It shouldn't have worked. Four men at the top, but they'd made it work.

"I sometimes think about … taking control myself."

"What do you mean?"

"Nothing. Forget I said anything."

She wasn't going to talk to me. Emily had been hurt too badly by those closest to her, and the only way to fix that kind of damage was to help heal her.

To help, I took hold of her hand, locking out fingers together. It wasn't much, but it was a start.

Chapter Eight

Emily

My driver not being there at the end of the day shouldn't have made me smile, but it did.

Gael, Caleb, River, and Vadik were waiting for me.

I also noticed half of the school had stuck around to see what was going on. They wanted to know everyone's business.

There were only three cars, which told me one of them rode with a friend.

"Seeing as Caleb and Vadik have already had kisses from you, I think it's only fair I take you on a journey," Gael said.

I held on to my bag. While waiting for my dad to be done screwing his latest mistress, I'd nearly spilled my dark secrets to Vadik. No matter how close they came, I wasn't going to let any of these guys know what I wanted out of life. What I used to hope for. They were nothing more than empty dreams with no way of ever seeing them through. I accepted that, which was why I had the trusty knife.

River had moved to Gael's car as well but he opted for a seat in the back.

"You're not planning on killing me, are you?" I asked.

"Not today." Gael winked. "Come on, beautiful. Have a little faith."

I rolled my eyes and stepped toward them. I let Gael take the bag, which he popped into the trunk of his car.

Bare without the protection, I climbed into the front seat, being careful to keep my skirt in place. I didn't want to live too dangerously.

"Stage one complete," he said, climbing behind the wheel. "Now, let's go and have some fun. I think it's time you learned to let loose."

I had a bad feeling about this.

Reaching for the door handle, intending to get out, I cried out as the locks kicked into place. Gael was already pulling away from the school.

I turned in my seat to see River holding the tip of a blade against his thigh.

"That's dangerous," I said.

"It's not the first time I'd have stabbed myself and it's not going to be the last." He winked at me. "But I love that you care."

Vadik and Caleb were following us.

"So, tell me, Emily. What's the most exciting thing you've ever done?" Gael asked.

"Nothing."

"I'm going to guess killing that guy, right?" Gael glanced at me. "If you've got nothing else, it had to be that loser."

"Do you have a point to this?" I reach out and grab the door handle.

He pressed his foot to the gas, overtaking a minivan and a bus on a very narrow piece of road.

We drove out of the town. I saw the signpost wishing us goodbye and to come back soon. Most towns had them. I couldn't imagine anyone wanting to live in Crude Hill for the rest of their lives, not with the people there.

Closing my eyes, I felt sick, but Gael wasn't done. He spun the car around, twisting us across the dirt embankment, coming to a sudden stop, and making me hit the side of the car.

When I was finally able to open my eyes, I was

so freaking angry. I started to hit him. Once, or twice wasn't enough. Removing my seat belt, I turned and began using my fists, but again, I felt like there was too much distance.

Without thinking, I crawled over across the gap and started to hit him some more, only to stop when I realized something hard pressed between my thighs. Gael had stopped trying to block me and instead, held on to my hips. There was no mistaking the hard cock touching me, and he wasn't even trying to hide it. Holy shit.

How did I get myself in this predicament?

Staring at him now, I couldn't really think.

I'd thought about death so often. It was like a favorite pastime for me. It was how I gained power away from my dad. If I was thinking about dying anyway, it meant I wouldn't put up as much of a fight. I'd focus and I would see an out. I wouldn't scream or beg, even though that would be logical. I did scream when the pain got to be too much, but that was merely down to a physical reaction. It didn't mean I wanted to actually do that.

Gael's grip got a little firmer on my body. I shouldn't like this. Just like I shouldn't have liked the kiss Caleb had given me. Anyone who touched me like they owned me, I should naturally hate, and yet, here I was, grinding myself on top of him, loving every second of it. This was a giant mistake. My dad would kill me.

The doctor would give a reason for him to hurt me some more. No doubt about it. I was under no illusions that even if I felt I had some control, my dad did. Killing myself was a last resort.

Neither of us moved or spoke.

His breathing sounded heavy. Did I even want to move? I wasn't sure what the answer was because the truth was my heart raced so fast. What would it hurt to just enjoy this? Would it really be so bad? There was no way this would lead to sex, so the doctor could do his exam, and I'd feel smug in knowing I'd had some fun at least.

****

Gael

Well, fuck me.

Damn.

This woman has some amazing hips on her. Not to mention how good she felt straddled across my lap. In my time, I'd had a lot of chicks in this position. Admittedly, none of them had made me feel like Emily. They hadn't killed someone for me. Emily was different. She'd taken a life all for me, and that kind of action deserved loyalty, even if she did fight it.

There was a darkness inside her. We all could see it.

She didn't want to see all the pretties and pretend like was fucking normal. No, we were all past that. We saw the pain and suffering in the world. We were the true monsters in this world, and there was no way we could get past that. I didn't want to.

I liked to hurt people.

My favorite thing was to humiliate them. Like Lauren, I had no desire for her. She was easy, but putting her in her place, showing the entire cafeteria she wasn't worthy of the Monsters was the fun part.

"I need to move," she said.

I wouldn't let her. Tightening my grip, I nudged my pelvis up against her. It wouldn't be long before we were joined anyway, and I didn't see a better way to enjoy this moment than with her inches from my dick.

"Why the rush?"

"I don't know what game you're playing, Gael.

Do not use me."

"Have you ever thought about using me? Playing some game? Your father can get his doctor all he wants, but there are other games to be had."

"There's way more to life than sex."

She wriggled again and I groaned in response.

"Will you stop that?"

"What? Enjoying how close your pussy is to my dick?" I moved my hands to the top of her thighs, sliding up the skirt.

Her father thought he was keeping some kind of control over her by making her wear dresses and skirts, but in truth, he was making her so much more vulnerable. I liked it.

When my hands touched skin, I moaned.

She glared at me. Her hands went to my wrists in an attempt to stop me, but her grip was shit.

I slid my hands up. "I bet you're soaking wet."

"Gael!"

That wasn't the correct response. If she told me no, I'd stop. I was many things, but a rapist wasn't one of them. When it came to women, forcing them wasn't my deal. None of us had that in us.

Sure, we could scare some chicks, make them think we were capable, but we weren't. It was what made us different, but there were a lot of other things we could do.

"What's the matter, Emily? Am I scaring you?"

"You don't scare me."

"No? Then what do I do? Do you want me?" I nudged my cock against her again, but this time, I covered her panties with my hand. I couldn't help but smile. They were wet. "Well, well, well, what do we have here?"

She slapped my chest but I pressed my thumb

against her clit. She gasped, crying out. Her eyes closed and her head tilted back. She looked so fucking sexy.

I wanted to fuck her, was desperate to.

But until I knew for sure it wouldn't get other of us killed, I was going to have to enjoy playing.

In the distance, I saw the cars coming closer.

I didn't want her distracted. Reaching out, I put the radio on, having some song blast loud over the noise of the engines approaching.

Slipping my fingers beneath the fabric of her panties, I grazed over her pussy, and she whimpered.

So wet.

Her eyes were still closed. Her teeth sinking into her lip. The hands that had tried to shove me now gripped my shirt, and all I'd done was put my thumb against her clit. With her cheeks flushed, the temptation to say screw it to all the shit with the law within our circles was so strong.

She was spoken for. Until our parents dealt with that problem, my father had asked me to just protect her.

I wanted to do more than protect her. I wanted to slide into her juicy pussy, take that cherry for my own. Glancing past my shoulder, I saw all three of my friends' faces. They wanted the exact same thing. Right now, they all wished they were with me. I could imagine Caleb's tight knuckles on the steering wheel, wondering just how tight her pussy was. I wouldn't find out today.

Slowly, I moved my thumb across her clit, watching her face as she started to move against my hand. Did she even realize how she responded to my touch? How good she looked?

Damn, if this was a prelude to who she'd be when I could fuck her, I couldn't wait. I wanted her so badly. Tonight, I'd be taking care of myself.

She whimpered and even though the radio was

loud, I heard it.

With my other hand, I went to the buttons of her shirt and started to unbutton them.

"No," she said.

She let me go long enough to hold her shirt together.

"I wouldn't hurt you." Pressing on her nub, I rocked my thumb back and forth across her clit.

Those teeth sank a little harder into her bottom lip.

"Trust me, Emily."

"I don't know you."

"But you could get to know me. I'm a really nice guy, and you'd like me a lot." I was far from nice, but she didn't need to know that. There was so much I wanted to do to her. To fuck her. To claim her. To make her mine.

But in the back of my mind, I knew I wanted to see her with Caleb, Vadik, and River. For a long time, I knew I was fucked up in the head. I wasn't like other people. I wanted my woman to come apart in my arms. To give herself over to me, but I also loved my friends so passionately that I wanted my woman to be with them.

So fucking sick and twisted, but it was one of the reasons we shared.

I didn't know their reasonings. I knew I would love to see her come apart. To finally let go and to just be completely taken over by sex, fucking, all of it.

I may be eighteen years old, but I knew how I liked my sex. I liked it dirty and hard. There was nothing clean or nice about it. Sex wasn't about turning the light off.

Emily didn't stop me as I unbuttoned her shirt. Each plastic piece giving way, exposing more of her skin until I saw the plainness of her very virginal bra. At least it had a catch on the front, which I took care of with a single flick of the wrist.

I was under no doubt that once she came, and when that high she was riding right now disappeared, I'd suffer for it. For now, it would all be worth it. Anything that meant I got a piece of her would always be worth it.

"Oh, fuck!" The curse fell from her lips.

I saw the change in her body, so I quickly moved the bra cup out of my way, seeing her beautiful tits for only the second time. They were as perfect as I remembered. So full and ripe.

I'd never given a fuck about how big nipples were or what color they were. Emily was different in every single way, and I loved every single part of her. The beauty of her was all for me at this very moment. I was the envy of my friends, and I didn't care.

Having this woman ride my hand until she came was all I wanted.

Leaning forward, I flicked one of her plump nipples before sucking it into my mouth, hearing her cry out.

She exploded. Her body rode my hand as she started to come and did so hard.

Pretty, so fucking pretty.

I didn't let go of her breast. Even as she whimpered, clearly finding it a little difficult to ride out her release, I made her go a little more. She had no idea just how amazing she was or what her body was capable of. When she couldn't take another second, I eased my touch until my hand lay flat against her.

"I can't believe you did that," she said, her voice sounding a little hoarse. She panted for breath.

"You liked it."

"And you think putting the radio on stopped me from knowing your friends were watching?"

She grabbed her bra, sliding the catch back into place, and I smiled at her. For my effort, she slapped my chest. "I fucking hate you."

"No, you don't." I grabbed her ass and lifted up her skirt, cupping those cheeks. She didn't even wear a thong.

"Stop it."

"Why? You know they want to see you."

She reached behind her and shoved the skirt down. "I don't think you're funny. None of this is funny."

"It is to me." I winked at her.

She hit me again and turned, sitting down, buttoning up her shirt. "Take me home."

"In a minute." I opened my car door then slammed it closed.

Caleb, River, and Vadik had all climbed out of their cars and leaned against the trunk. River was the only one with a smile on his face.

I held my hands up. "She didn't tell me to stop!"

"Stop looking so smug."

I couldn't wipe the smile off my face though. I was the first one out of our group to bring her to orgasm.

"Wait until you see how beautiful she looks. Nothing is fake about her. She's not trying to impress us."

"I'm standing right here," Emily said.

I glanced behind me to see she stood there, now fully composed. Her uniform in place. The only sign that something wasn't completely right within her world was the blush on her cheeks.

She wasn't fooling anyone.

"Are you taking me home or are you determined to get me killed?"

Caleb pointed at his car while Vadik shook his

head at me.

She moved toward the back door, climbing in.

"You don't fool me, Emily. You could have stopped me any time. All you had to do was say the words."

She looked at me as if she wanted to kill me. I had to wonder if she'd be pissed if I mentioned how cute she looked. I kept that piece of information to myself, but it was true. She looked cute.

She climbed into the car and slammed the door closed.

"I'll take her home," Caleb said.

River looked between Vadik and me and then settled on moving toward me.

"See you guys later." I wanted nothing more than to claim a kiss from her, but I knew there was no chance of that.

I'd made her come and she was already pissed at herself for allowing me so close. One day soon, I was going to have it all. I'd have my dick balls deep within her and those lips on mine.

Caleb climbed into the car, pulled back onto the road, and left us all behind.

I turned over my ignition, slamming my door closed, and followed.

"So how was it?" River asked.

"You really want to know?"

"I wouldn't ask if I didn't want to know."

"She's so fucking perfect," I said. "When you get her in your arms, you'll know what I mean. She's fire and ice, and everything that's perfect in the world."

I couldn't deny it. She was everything and then more. This was only the start. As far as I was concerned, Emily may belong to someone else at this point on a contract, but in truth, she was a Monster, and we were going to claim her regardless. Consequences be damned.

Chapter Nine

Emily

Even though I came in Gael's lap, or more accurately, on his lap, for the rest of the week, school was uneventful. That was the truth. It was like none of the chaos or commotion had happened.

They were in all of my classes, apart from art class. Just Vadik was there, but he didn't invade my space. I had to wonder why. He knew I was shit at drawing or creating. The teacher had forced us all to draw what we considered a tree should look like. Where some of the class went for autumnal colors, with the leaves on the ground as if a gust of wind had swept them away, others did tress in full summer bloom. I did a thick trunk, and then some lines to give way to branches. That was it.

I didn't have a single artistic bone in my body. I knew it, Vadik knew it, the entire class knew it. Yet, the teacher told me I put others to shame.

In answer, I walked right out the door. There was no fucking way I was listening to her bullshit.

I went straight to the bathroom, which was empty. Sometimes there were girls hanging out, or fucking was going on. A virgin I may be, but if my eyes were the judge of said innocence, I'd be far from it.

Running some water, I splashed it onto my face. I didn't know what was worse right now. The tension at home was at a whole new level. My mom was coherent once again, and trying to play the perfect doting mom. When I got in, because my dad had a little less control over my body by bruising it, he'd instead started to pay extra attention to my classwork. I now had to study in his office. He never had any important phone calls, but there was a desk set up so he could keep an eye on me.

I no longer had the luxury of being in my room with my back to the wall.

My dad knew my problems, and he'd made it so there was space behind me. He had a secret door that I had yet to identify, but it was where my brother appeared from so many times. I knew my dad was playing with my head. He got off on making me feel less than him.

"You okay?" Vadik asked.

A laugh escaped my lips. Turning off the water, I grabbed some of the tissues and dried my face.

"This is the girls' bathroom."

"You think I haven't seen inside this room before?"

I rolled my eyes. "Of course you have."

"No one believes her," he said. "They all know who's paying for her jewelry and pretty things."

"I don't give a shit."

"Running out of a class doesn't exactly make me believe you."

"You think I care about what you believe?"

"I think you do, yes."

"Well, you're wrong." I threw the tissues into the trash. Sure enough, there was a used condom in the bottom.

This school. Was it like this at normal schools?

"What do you want, Vadik? Why did you follow me?"

"Is it so hard to believe I wanted to make sure you're okay?"

"Yes, it is. You think I don't know that every single person has an agenda here? I know it. I get it even. How could I not? It's not like we all keep it a secret we want to kill each other. We all have a death wish."

My words echoed around the room. Or did they

just go off in my head?

Vadik allowed the door to close and he advanced toward me. I took a step back, not liking how threatening he seemed. Even as he closed the distance between us, my pussy instantly went wet.

My heart pounded.

None of this was fear, but anticipation. What would he do?

I was trapped between his body and the sink.

His hand went to my hip. "Do you have a death wish?"

"I don't know what you're talking about."

"You do. Don't play dumb. It doesn't suit you."

I glared at him. It was none of his business what I thought, felt, or did. "What really needs to happen is you and the rest of your friends leave me alone."

He tilted his head to the side. "You don't like being the center of attention?"

"No." It was the truth. Overnight, I'd become the envy of the school. Girls looked at me with equal measures of adoration and disdain. I didn't care. The guys, they wanted to know what it was about me that had the guys so curious. They were more interested in what their dick wanted.

I couldn't give a shit what any of them wanted.

My peace. My freedom, what little I had, was gone. I hadn't been able to hang out at the library.

Since the day I let Gael touch me in the car, there had been a driver at school to take me home to hell.

Between their attention at school and what I had to deal with at home, I was at a breaking point. To survive, I needed to be cautious. At any point, I could end up dead.

Not that death was such a huge problem.

The sad truth was I looked forward to it. There

were moments I thought about pushing my father to the next level. He couldn't have his precious money or deal if he killed me. I'd love to know I fucked up his life because he ended mine.

I needed to get my shit together because that wasn't fucking funny.

"You're going to have to get used to it." The hand on my hip wasn't bruising. He stroked me through the fabric of my uniform.

Licking my dry lips, I knew it was completely messed up how I was reacting to him, to them all. They were all best friends. Being in a relationship with them was crazy. So messed up. It couldn't happen.

I put my hand over his. "You've got to back off."

"No, I don't have to do anything I don't want to." The hand on my hip slid up, going toward my chest. His thumb brushed underneath my tits.

I drew in deep breaths, very much aware of how close he was to me.

He'd closed the distance. The tips of his boots brushed mine.

"Do you think I don't see the pain inside you, Emily? You can't draw for shit, but there's something about a piece of art, no matter how good or bad the artist is. You're in pain. You feel like you're drowning. You hate me, Caleb, River, and Gael. I bet your hatred of him is even worse, isn't it?"

"I don't know what you're talking about."

"Oh, you do, believe me. You do." He smiled, but it wasn't nice. This was deadly, dangerous.

I hadn't seen this side of Vadik.

"You hate Gael because he broke past those feelings inside you. The ones where you think death would be so easy, and it will. I know what you think and how you feel. If you think you're alone, you're wrong.

We all know how easy and fucked-up it would be. What you hate most about Gael is even as you want to hate us, he awakened your curiosity. You now want him, even though you also want to hate him."

I shook my head. "I've got to get back to class."

His hand cupped my tit. My nipple pressed against the palm of his hand. "You don't have to do anything you don't want to."

None of what he was saying made any sense.

He let go of my breast, but he suddenly gripped my ass with both of his hands before one slid up my back, cupping my head, drawing me down, and he was kissing me hard. His tongue traced out, curving over my lips, then plunged inside my mouth.

The kiss felt amazing.

I didn't push him away. Holding his face between my hands, I gave up fighting and kissed him back, not wanting him to stop.

He growled against my lips and I did no more than wrap my legs around his waist. I hated that he was right.

Gael had awakened something in me.

My virginity. My precious fucking virginity was something my father wanted for his own deals. For me, at this very moment, I wanted to say to hell with all of it, to lose it right here, right now, in the girls' bathroom at Crude Hill High.

Only, Vadik pulled away.

I glanced down and saw his cock pressed against the front of his pants.

"What game are you guys playing?" I asked.

Vadik looked at me. There were no questions, just a stare.

"You and Gael. I haven't forgotten Caleb either. Is this where you all make me want you? Where I make a fool out of myself, only to have Gael push me aside as if I'm nothing?"

"You're not very trustworthy, are you?"

"Give me a good reason why I should be." I jumped off the sink.

"We're not playing a game with you."

"Then why are you all kissing me?"

"Has it ever occurred to you that maybe we all want to kiss you?"

I laughed. I couldn't help it. "Really? Look, I've seen some of the girls who go to this school and I know I'm nothing special."

He raised a brow.

"I'm not looking for compliments."

Vadik smiled and stepped back.

"No, you explain this to me."

"Why explain it to you when it will be a lot more fun to show you?" He winked at me and left the girls' bathroom.

I kicked the base of the sink. "Fuck!"

Staring at my reflection, I didn't look happy. Far from it. My lips were swollen from his kiss. My cheeks red. I didn't even recognize myself.

Closing my eyes, I counted to three, then to six, then to ten.

Finally, when I'd gained my control again, I left the bathroom and went back to art. No one looked at me. Vadik was still drawing. I happened to notice the teacher didn't get too close to him or his work. She nodded her head. "Wonderful."

He shot her a glare and she scurried away.

She came right toward me.

"Emily, do you want to talk about what happened?" she asked.

I turned toward her. All I wanted to do was

scream at her, tell her what a waste of space she was. How my father would never leave my mother, and she was spreading her legs for the wrong man.

Instead, I was the good girl.

Years upon years of practice brought a smile to my lips as if nothing mattered.

"You do have some talent, Emily." She patted my shoulder and once again, I counted in my head.

I turned back to my tree. This wasn't talent.

I hated drawing.

I hated school.

I hated my father.

My life.

All of it.

But what I didn't hate was the way Vadik looked at me. The way Gael touched me, as if I belonged to him already. The kiss Caleb had taken, his ownership. Even River's understanding.

All four of them had made me feel and I didn't want that. My life was already over before it had begun, and each of these guys had woken me up. Now, I feared I was never going to be able to sleep again.

My heart beat in anticipation.

Hope bloomed within my chest.

Life no longer seemed unbearable. But now that I'd thought all of this, I didn't know if I was going to be able to handle what might happen when all of this fell apart, which it would. There was no doubt about it.

This between us was a ticking time bomb, and one day soon, it was going to go off.

****

Caleb

This wasn't the first murder I'd seen.

I stood watching as my father's men threw the

body into the water. It wouldn't be long before the creatures of the ocean tore his body apart, feeding on the traitor's flesh.

My father, Daniel, sat back, a glass of wine in his hand as he smiled. "Now that's a job well done."

I didn't say anything.

This wasn't the first time I'd been taken on one of his little expeditions. It was late on a Saturday night. This was where my father did his business with rats or traitors. First, they'd be taken to a warehouse where for many hours, one of our men would get every single word or secret past his lips. Death wouldn't come easily.

Teeth, fingernails, and toenails would be removed. Then nipples and other pieces of flesh would come. Fingers were next.

Slowly, piece by piece, they'd be removed until all that remained was a carcass.

I'd seen the torture process many times. My first happened when I was twelve years old. Daniel believed no son of his would have a weak stomach. The first one, I vomited, and he made me clean up the vomit, blood, and shit afterward. The stench had stayed with me for weeks, even though I had scrubbed my body raw.

The second one, I didn't throw up.

By the fourth, my dad wanted me to join in.

I knew we didn't have the best of parents. None of us did. Our fathers all had their own methods of making us the men who would one day take over from them. You'd think with the constant example we made of men and women who tried to rat, there wouldn't be so many. There was always someone who grew a conscience, and that meant we got to feed the fishes.

"How's school?" my father asked.

I looked at him, brow raised. "You really want to know about school?"

He laughed.

"You know everything already. If you've got a question, ask."

"Be careful how you speak to me, Caleb. You may be my son, but I have no problems putting you in your place."

My dad had no trouble hurting me. He took great pride in how much shit I took from him.

I nodded, letting him know I was sorry. To say the words aloud showed weakness.

"So, the girl, Emily. Tell me about her."

"What's there to tell?"

"I wasn't born yesterday. I've got eyes and ears everywhere. She's become the Monsters' shiny new toy. I take it her cherry hasn't been popped."

My hands clenched into fists. "She's still intact," I said.

"Good."

"Why does it matter?"

"This deal her father has, it intrigues us. In fact, we're setting up a gala. It's a nice affair, a charity event. We're inviting everyone, including Emily's betrothed. It will be a good opportunity to see how Crane reacts. I don't like what I'm hearing."

"You think he's trying to take over?"

He tapped his fingers on the arm of his chair. The tension mounted as he looked at me. I may be his son, but he also only allowed me to know what he believed my rank entitled me. There was a lot of stuff I didn't know, or at least, he thought I didn't know.

I wasn't a fool. I hadn't been for a long time.

I knew how our world worked.

You didn't get beaten black and blue without learning a thing or two. My father was my ally and my enemy.

"Something stinks with Crane. We're not exactly sure." He pursed his lips. "For a man who is merely a minion, he has a lot of offshore accounts." Daniel chuckled. "He thinks he's good at hiding things, but he clearly underestimates us. What does the girl mean to you?"

This time, I stared at my father. He wasn't an idiot.

For me and the guys to pay special attention to one girl, it meant something. My dad had a lot of spies everywhere. I was always careful. All of the guys were.

"Why haven't you dealt with Crane?" I asked.

Daniel smiled. At this moment, he wasn't a father, but a boss. "You answer my question first."

"You always taught me to get the information I want."

"I'm not your enemy, son, at least not yet. I've been rather lenient. You should respect what I've given you so far."

And I knew without a fact, he'd punish me if I crossed the line. He'd given me plenty of chances, but he wasn't going to keep allowing me to get away with things. Not when the reputation of the Monsters was at stake.

"She's important," I said.

He sipped at his wine. "You know, we were a lot like you guys at one point. We were unbreakable. We took what we wanted and to hell with the consequences. Of course, we also had to live in a school where people died on a regular basis. To some, the kind of school system you have now makes you all weak. There's nothing wrong with sleeping with one eye open." He paused. "Whatever this is with Emily, it will be for fun only, Caleb."

I gritted my teeth but didn't say anything to

dispute him.

"One girl to four boys, it's not going to work."

"And if it could?" I asked. I knew how fucked up our needs were. We didn't want to have multiple women. That would mess us up. The fact all four of us were attracted to Emily was a damn good start.

Daniel laughed. "It won't. You're all behaving like boys and that's never a good combination when it comes to a woman. For now, she has way too much power over you. What will you do if she starts finding Vadik more enjoyable? Or picking River's company over yours? The jealousy is a disease in our family, Caleb. You can't risk it. None of you can."

"And you know about those feelings?"

"There are a lot of things you don't know about us, Caleb. Don't for a second believe I give you this warning without prior knowledge." Daniel stood and threw the remains of his wine across the deck.

I hated coming onto the boat. I never liked how it rocked. I preferred to have something steady and sturdy beneath my feet.

"I want to meet the betrothed. I want to know exactly what's going on with Crane. It's rare for an engagement to get past me."

"Emily doesn't know about it."

"She will soon enough. It's time we headed back to the house." He moved to go into the main deck.

"Dad, how do you know it won't work?" I asked. I didn't want to continue having this conversation, but I saw no other choice.

Daniel sighed. "There are secrets even you can't know the answer to."

That was it.

He closed the door, leaving me out in the cold.

I didn't mind.

Sitting in his chair, I watched the water as we moved, heading back toward the bay where our cars were parked.

By the time I sat in the car, my dad was already on the phone organizing a replacement for the man they just killed. We didn't go straight home. We stopped at an abandoned garage. My dad and two of his guards climbed out, holding a briefcase.

I watched the swap happen, the handshake, and then my dad was back inside.

"Crooked cops. I tell you, they're worse than the criminals."

I recognized the cop. He'd been to the school a few times when there was a sudden raid on the lockers to check and see if drugs were being distributed. It only ever happened when there was suspicion an outsider's product had been brought into the fold. The consequences were dire.

Once we arrived home, I stepped into the main foyer and saw my mother at the bottom of the stairs. She offered my dad a smile, but he didn't return it.

I frowned as I watched them.

My parents' troubled marriage wasn't news to me. I was very much aware they had troubles but I knew my mother loved my dad. I didn't understand why. He was a total bastard to her, and without remorse.

I didn't linger. There was no point. As I step toward the stairs, my mother, Molly, smiled at me.

"Are you okay, sweetheart?" she asked. She went to touch my face but hesitated.

"I'm fine."

I made my way upstairs to my bedroom, closing the door. I removed my jacket, kicked off my boots, and went to my knife and the target in the corner. Ever since River had started practicing two years ago, I'd made it my mission to be better than him.

All four of us would one day be in charge, but to the outside world, my dad, like me, would be the leaders. I was older than my friends by a day, if that. It was how we always were. United. Never divided.

There were times we didn't know if we were really friends, or we just didn't know any other way.

I'd die for all of them.

I picked up the knife, stepped away from the target, lined up, and threw. I had three knives that I practiced with. One after the other, I impaled them into my target.

The satisfaction of training didn't even help me to clear my troubled thoughts.

I put the knives down and instead, went to my bed, lying down to stare up at the ceiling. If my dad knew what we were planning and how it would end, did it mean all of our dads at one point had fallen for one woman?

No, it wasn't possible.

If there was going to be any evidence of our dads falling for one woman, it would be in the albums my dad kept in the library. I rarely looked through old pictures of myself or my friends as babies or into teenagers. There was no point. I didn't believe in looking back.

My interest was piqued, though, and even as I hated myself, I got to my feet and padded down to the library.

It was dark, so I went to the table lamp and turned it on. The albums were lined up on the far wall. The scent of musty old books never appealed to me. I didn't understand Emily's fascination with the library.

Crouching down, I ran my finger down the spine of each book, finding the one dated the year I was born.

I pulled the book out, sat on my ass, and flicked

the file open. There weren't many pictures here. Barely any.

I frowned as I looked, though. The pictures I looked at were ones I'd seen a few times. When the guys come over and get all nostalgic, they get the books out. I stared at the picture of us in the crib. I'd been referred to as a fat baby. I was bigger than my friends. I got to my feet and moved over to the lamp, putting the picture beneath so I could get a good, proper look at it.

There was no fucking way I was a fat baby. I didn't know a lot about newborns, but I did know for a fact they weren't able to sit up straight. If that was me, then it was really fucking clear to me that I was older than a newborn.

Rather than put the picture away, I slid it into my pocket. My dad may have made a passing comment, but I wanted to know the truth, and there was no way I was letting him get away with keeping me in the dark.

Chapter Ten

River

I'd never considered myself the kind of person who would stalk someone. Yet, here I stood in Emily's room like one. It wasn't too hard getting into her bedroom. I'd seen her looking out the window a few nights ago, and there was a kitchen around back that the cook liked to keep the door open while she worked. There was also a guard who liked to get the extra food.

I'd stood in the garden and watched for the past couple of evenings in the same routine. Tonight, I decided to play a game of chance and take one. Now, I stood in her bedroom. The scent of her was everywhere.

Sitting on the edge of her bed, I checked the level of bounce. A rather nice bed. I was pleased to know her parents took care of her.

Her bedroom screamed her, which was odd. Her desk had her back to the wall, facing the main door but also keeping the window in view.

Getting to my feet, I pulled her curtains closed and switched on her bedside lamp.

If the guys could see me now, they'd think I was going crazy. They wouldn't be wrong. I didn't care about a girl's bedroom.

Emily had slid onto our radar, and like my friends, I couldn't seem to get her out of my mind. Not that I wanted to.

When I heard footsteps coming toward her bedroom, I hid in the closet, not wanting to give away my position, at least not yet. My dad told me to lay low when it came to Emily. They were working out the Crane problem. There was only one issue I saw, that he was bargaining Emily off to a stranger without first consulting his bosses. That was a bad idea.

"I checked her laundry basket, Anne. You don't have to go in there," a woman said.

"I have to check. You know what he's like." Through the doorway, I saw a redhead and a brunette enter the room. They were dressed in maid's uniforms.

"I don't know why. He keeps her in his office now. I can't believe we have to bring her underwear to him. It's freaky," the brunette said.

"Don't let anyone hear you say that."

"It's weird, Anne. Come on. If your dad asked to see your underwear at the end of each day?"

"She doesn't know," Anne said.

"Poor girl."

"Look at the life she lives, Lee. She's not hurting for a good life."

Lee snorted. "This is a good life? Look at the way she moves her bedroom. She's terrified. I've seen the bruises on her and I've heard her crying. She's all alone here. We have better lives. What he makes her go through… You may not feel for her, but I do. I care."

"Yeah, well, she's going to be a rich wife, and we'll be nothing but washed-up old maids. You're right, no panties."

"What do you think he does with the panties?" Lee asked. "Sniffs them or something?"

"Ew, gross. I don't know. Don't care. He's obsessed with her staying a virgin and I hear the Monsters are sniffing around her. It has him even more pissed."

They left the bedroom and I stepped out of the closet.

Wow. Fucking wow.

I'd been kidnapped. Trapped. Unable to get out. Tortured, close to death, but I didn't know what was worse. Knowing I was going to die, or living a life I didn't know if there was any out of.

Emily lived this life every single day.

She got up knowing there was going to be pain. Waiting to see what her father would do next. It was why she never had friends. She kept to herself.

I moved toward the bed, resting my feet up, and looked over at her drawer.

In my hand, I already held the blade she had used to save Gael.

Out of curiosity, I opened the drawer and found some notebooks. I picked one up and flicked it open. It was blank.

The one underneath, I opened that to find a literal diary of her day. Going to class, what she studied. It was more of a monologue of activity. *I went to English. We read Shakespeare. A couple guys said something stupid. Bell rang.* There was no flow, and I knew she could write.

This was clearly done because she knew even in her own personal thoughts, she wasn't alone. Her dad had people watching every single moment. I didn't know how she could cope with that.

Closing the book, I was about to put it back in when the recognizable point of a blade caught my attention. It was beneath a few other things wrapped in some cloth. I pulled it out and looked at it.

There was something about the blade that captured my attention. I didn't know what it was.

She had a knife on her in school. Now she had one next to where she slept at night.

Why did she have it? For what purpose? With the bruises I'd caught sight of, she could have killed her father or brother, given the chance.

I heard the footsteps approaching, but I made no

move to put the blade away.

Emily stepped into her bedroom, pausing when she saw me. Her face went pale and she looked behind her before closing the door.

"What the hell are you doing?" she asked, whispering.

I held up the knife. "What is this?" I asked.

"Is this any of your business?" She rushed toward me as if to take the blade off me, but I held it out of her reach.

"Don't be a dick," she said.

"You use some naughty words. Does your dad know how bad you are?"

She glared at me and tried to reach. I moved, nudging her hand out of the way so she had no choice but to collapse on top of me. Her curvy body pressed to mine, and I couldn't handle it, so I rolled her until she lay beneath me.

I dropped her blade to the bed and smirked down at her. "Well, well, well, this is a rather interesting position."

"This isn't funny." She wriggled beneath me. "Let me go."

"No."

"If my father catches you here, you're going to be dead."

"And start a war with my dad?" I tut. "No one's that stupid. Unless you believe your dad has a death wish. Keep on moving. I love it." I pressed my hard cock between her thighs. I thought about those women coming into her room, invading her privacy, and it pissed me off.

"This isn't funny, River. Why are you here?" she asked.

At first, she was tense, refusing to give me an inch. Slowly, she relaxed beneath me. I held her hands down to the bed, keeping her locked in place.

"That's not so hard, is it?"

"I don't know what game you're playing and I don't like it."

I sighed. "I'm not playing a game. Why do you have a knife?"

"For protection."

"Emily, I saw the damage you did. If you had a knife to protect yourself, why don't you ever use it?"

"I don't know who you think you are. Sneaking into my bedroom puts you on the weirdo scale. You know that, right? I'm sick and tired of all of you. Leave me alone."

I pressed my hips between her thighs and she gasped. "I don't think you want us to leave you alone. In fact, I think you want us to be very, very naughty to you."

"You have no idea how wrong you are."

I laughed. I just couldn't help it.

She jerked her hands from beneath me and placed them over my mouth. "Please, I don't … he will hurt you."

"No one can hurt me."

"Damn it, River, you're not immortal."

"That you know of."

She rolled her eyes.

Flicking my tongue out, I stroked over her hand and she gasped, pulling her hand away.

"Why are you here?" she asked.

"I thought you could use some company. I was bored as well."

"Great, so you come here for your amusement." She tried to wriggle away.

"I came here to see you."

"Because you couldn't wait until school?"

I couldn't. I was bored and she was on my mind. "You know, I've been thinking about your face."

She frowned. "Why? You want to carve it up?"

"No, I was wondering how you looked when you came on Gael's fingers."

Her cheeks went bright red.

"I've never envied Gael anything. But I can't help but wonder how you look, or those tits as they shook when you came."

"River?"

I leaned in close and brushed my lips across her neck. I flicked my tongue over her pulse.

"I need to go and shower."

The instant I let my guard down, she took full advantage, running toward her bathroom.

I chuckled.

She could run all she wanted to.

I'd already checked and there was no lock on that door.

Sitting up, I felt the hard ridge of my cock pressing against my zipper. I waited for about two minutes, picked up my blade, and entered the bathroom. I always needed my knife on me or close for me to be able to threaten. I didn't like being alone. Without it, I was weak. I was one of the best when it came to fighting with a knife. I'd killed with it. I liked the artistry it required.

The door was closed. The steam filled up the bathroom. I saw the outline of her, and I just couldn't pass up this opportunity. I wasn't washed either. I needed to get clean.

Stripping out of my clothes, I didn't make too much noise.

I opened the shower door and she spun toward me, gasping, trying to cover her body to no avail. There was a lot of her to keep hidden. Big tits, a nice cunt. Gael had told me how sweet she was. He hadn't gotten a taste of her, but tonight, that was what I was going to do. He may have gotten the first orgasm, but I'd get the first taste.

"What the hell, River?"

I closed the shower door.

"Put that down," she said.

"You keep a blade near you because it gives you back the power, doesn't it?" I said.

"I have no idea what you're talking about."

"Oh, you do. You know everything I'm talking about. I'm right. You've probably had that knife with you for a long time. Maybe when the first punch came. Or was it a slap?"

She stared at me. Her hands were still covering her body and doing a bad job of it. She licked her lips. "It was a slap."

"Where?"

"Around the face. I wasn't expecting it and I landed on the floor hard. I hit my head. It was the first time it had ever happened."

"And you have the knife because you know the hits will keep on coming, and this is your way to keep your control. He can't keep taking from you. One day, you intend to take from him."

"I don't—"

I silenced her by slamming my lips down on hers. At first, she didn't respond, almost like she was a little unsure of what she was supposed to do. Seconds ticked by. Maybe even minutes, and finally, she responded.

She kissed me back, her hands going to my chest.

I wrapped my hands around her back, drawing her close, feeling her naked body pressed against mine. Fuck me, she was everything I thought she would be. The points of her nipples rubbed against my chest, begging for attention. My dick was so fucking hard and I wanted to be inside her. For now, I'd have to hold back. It was the last thing I wanted to do, but I'd do it for her.

Sliding my hands down to her ass, I cupped the rounded cheeks, feeling her moan against my lips.

I broke the kiss and trailed my lips down her neck to her pulse, licking her.

Slowly, her hands slid down my back, to my hips.

I waited to go to her pussy as she touched my cock. Her grip was uncertain and I loved that. I didn't want her to be completely sure with what she was doing. I liked her being hesitant, waiting for me.

Once, twice, she pumped my length. Even with her inexperience, I was so close to coming. I pushed her hand away and I sank to the floor of the shower.

"What are you doing?"

I lifted her foot, putting it on the ledge. Kissing the inside of her knee, I smirked up at her. "I think you already know."

She had fine hairs on the lips of her sex. I parted them with my fingers, and even though her entrance was what I wanted, I focused on her clit, tasting her for the first time. Her head tilted back and a cry erupted from her lips.

I couldn't help but look up at her as I licked her cunt. So pretty. All mine. She belonged to all of us, and even as I took this first, I couldn't wait for her to come on my friends' tongues as well. Damn, it would be even sexier if she came while I was balls deep inside her. Now that would be sexy as fuck.

It didn't take her long to come and when she did, I knew I would treasure this moment forever.

****

Emily

Crude Hill High was abuzz with anticipation. One for the ball the Monsters were throwing. Invites had been sent out, and my presence had been requested. There was no option to turn it down. I'd been given a direct order. Anyone else may be fucking terrified and I was like everyone else, because that was exactly what was happening. I was scared.

I didn't know if I'd be dead when the ball happened. My dad kept looking at me like he wanted to wring my neck. Sometimes I taunted him by keeping my neck exposed, just to tempt him.

I was going crazy.

First, I let Vadik kiss me in the girls' bathroom, wanting him to do a whole lot more. Then there was River who broke into my house and waited for me in my bedroom, where I let him lick my pussy. Not to mention what happened with Gael in his car. I didn't know what was going to happen next. My body was like a constant, tight ball of needs.

Caleb found reasons to randomly touch me.

Gael was always hinting at what he wanted to do to me. They were everywhere. Apart from today. They had to go out and do all of their manly stuff. I got to eat lunch, seated in my regular seat without being the center of attention, which brought us to the next buzz of attention.

The school had a brand-new student.

Ashley March. So far, not a lot of interest had happened. I'd seen her. A beautiful brunette with kind eyes, but and here was the big but, she was already considered an outcast. Not only was she not the biological child, she was the daughter of one of the minion's mistresses.

To the food chain within this school, it made her lower than Drake, and a lot of people wouldn't even help her. She'd arrived at three classes at the wrong time. Had been shoved into lockers.

I spotted her arriving at the cafeteria five minutes ago to the whispers of *whore*, *slut*, *bitch*, *cow*, and many other names.

I opened up my bottle of water and went back to reading the notes on a current assignment when a tray slid opposite me. I looked up and saw Ashley. Her smile was genuine.

"Hi, I hope it's okay for me to sit here."

"I really don't think that's a good idea."

Her smile remained in place and she nodded. Guilt ate away at me. This girl was in the deep end and heading in one direction, down. The sharks here wouldn't let her survive long. I didn't know why I felt this way. I'd seen newbies come and go, but Ashley was different. She wasn't one of us.

"Look, it's not you." I lifted my book. "I'm not good company. I don't have friends."

"Are you, er, are you like me?" She still hadn't sat down.

"I'm a girl, so I guess that makes us similar."

Her smile widened. "That's not what I mean and you know it." She sighed. "I mean, are you like, a mistress's kid?" She nibbled on her lips and I shook my head.

"I'm a minion's kid."

"Oh." She was all alone.

She wasn't a bastard, or a secret love child. She was a no one.

"Sit," I said. If I made this new friend, it might actually send the Monsters running in the opposite direction and I wouldn't have to worry about being disappointed when they lost interest in me.

"I don't … if you don't…"

I smiled at her. "Please, sit." I never smiled. In this place, turned-up lips meant weakness. I wasn't weak, but I also wasn't going to turn her away. Snapping my book closed, I stared at her. I didn't bother to see we'd become the topic of conversation. Not only was I considered a Monsters' whore, but I wasn't cavorting with the wrong crowd. What-fucking-ever.

They had to deal.

"I'm Ashley March," she said, holding her hand out.

"Emily Crane."

We shook hands.

Ashley glanced around the room. "I didn't realize a place like this exists. It looks like a normal school."

"Your mom tell you about this place?"

"My stepdad. I don't know if he is my stepdad. I don't know what to call him." She pressed her lips together. "I will understand if you want to bully me."

"Wow, okay, I don't do that. Not here. I don't bully. There's a difference between being a bully and surviving. I survive in this school and that's what you're going to need to do. Here, you're the lower being. You're something they want to crush. What you're going to need to do is show that you don't give a shit. Do you care?"

"What? That they all call me a whore and dirt, and want to smash my face in?" she asked. "Of course, it bothers me, but at my old school, I was called trash, so I guess it doesn't matter."

"What kind of school did you go to?" I asked. I shouldn't be learning more about this girl than I needed to.

"A normal one. You know, where jocks are just football players, and people are normal."

"We're all normal here. Just with a few added extras."

Ashley sighed. "It was a lot easier when my mom didn't fall in love with a guy with a few added extras." She pouted.

"Don't cry," I said. "Here, crying is the kiss of death. What you need to do is learn to have a backbone. They will hurt you here."

"See, this is what I'm talking about." Ashley shook her head. "I already miss being called trash. You know, I had a note in my locker telling me they were going to cut my face up."

I sighed and rubbed at my temple. "Do me a favor. Carry a weapon or mace, or something."

Ashley's eyes went wide. "You think they're telling the truth?"

"They don't make threats they don't keep. Sorry."

Her chest rose and fell. "I'm sorry. Just a lot to process right now."

"It's one of them. Take your time." I sat, spearing my fork into my fries and popping them into my mouth, chewing.

"So, do you have to fight for yourself as well?" she asked.

"I tend to go under the radar. Or I did until recently."

"What happened recently?" Ashley asked.

I didn't get a chance to respond as Lauren, who'd still been trying to deal with the very public rejection Gael had subjected her to, poured the gravy pot over Ashley's head.

Laughter filled the room. I hadn't been paying attention. Otherwise, I could have stopped that.

Lauren looked toward the room, wanting their respect again.

I never got involved. I always stayed in my own quiet corner. One moment, I was sitting with my back against my trusty wall, the next, my lunch was across the table as I lifted up my tray. Before she could react, I had hit her across the face with the metal.

Silence met my outburst and Lauren went down, blood instantly spurting from her nose.

My heart raced, but I had this twisted sense of satisfaction. Then, while she was still down, I grabbed the trash bin and, fuck, it was empty, but I wasn't done. I lifted it up, and all the scraps dropped out onto her.

I didn't know if Ashley was crying, but I didn't care.

"You're nothing but trash, Lauren. Don't ever forget your place or Gael may have to put you back in it."

I grabbed Ashley's hand, and I didn't scamper out of the back door. I led her across the dining room.

No one at this time would touch me. Not while they know the Monsters were my allies.

I left the cafeteria and took her to the gym shower.

She was crying.

"Don't cry," I said.

"I'm sorry. But, what the hell? He paid a fortune for this uniform and look what they've done."

"You'll be fine." I went to the supply closet where spare uniforms were kept. I grabbed replacements but then I saw she was still standing there with her arms wrapped around herself, clearly trying to protect herself. "I know the gravy isn't that great. Come on. You don't want to be stinking of it all day. It's horrible stuff."

She was still crying.

"Don't cry," I repeated. "They'll know they're getting to you and that's never good. You've got to be a fighter here."

"I'm not a fighter."

"You're in the deep end, Ash, you've got to do something." I pushed her into the shower, keeping out of the way as the water cascaded over her head. I didn't even know why I was helping her. There was nothing I can do. My dad would have a fit if he knew I was helping a no one.

"I didn't want to come here."

"No one ever wants to come here. This is what we do though. We find a way around it."

"This is what you did?"

"It's what we all do, Ash. Don't let them get to you. Come on. Get out of those clothes."

She sniffled and I waited.

I wasn't going to strip her out of her clothes. This was the fight she needed.

"I can't believe you hit that girl with your food tray."

I thought about the way she sat on Gael's lap several weeks ago. "She deserved it."

"I don't think anyone deserves to be hit."

I didn't say anything else. This girl, I didn't know where she came from, but it was clear she wasn't from around here. She certainly wasn't a part of the life either. This world wasn't for her, not even by a little bit.

"Thank you," she said.

I turned to see she'd stripped out of her gravy-stained clothes. "What for?"

"For not abandoning me. I … I don't know what I'm doing."

I should leave. This wasn't my fight and I was already trying to make it through high school. The Monsters had made it a lot easier for me, but I couldn't seem to move. Folding my arms across my chest, I nodded. "No problem. You've got to learn to protect yourself."

"We're not supposed to have to protect ourselves in school."

I blew out a breath. "This isn't like any other school, Ash. You've got to learn fast, or next time, it won't be gravy they're pouring over your head."

Chapter Eleven

Vadik

Blood was on my hands.

Blood covered all of our hands. Not right now, but I knew it was there. I counted my victims. Today, my personal death count rose to fifteen.

I sat outside on one of the many benches my father had installed. The truth was I wanted to go and find Emily. Everywhere I turned, arrangements were being made for this fucked-up ball. I didn't like it.

It wouldn't be long before I met Emily's betrothed. She had no idea her father had sold her.

"You okay?" Caleb asked, walking toward me.

"Yeah, I'm good."

"How come you didn't turn up?"

Normally, after a raid and kill, I would go hang out with Caleb. We'd talk about bullshit and it would make me happy.

"Didn't feel like it."

I hated killing people. Caleb knew that about me, and I thought, in a way, he understood, but at the same time, he also wasn't quite on board with my reasoning for it. Some of the lives we'd taken, they'd been innocents. With my hands resting on my thighs, I didn't see what was in front of me, but I saw the wife of one of the men who tried to report us to the police. He'd been working for my father and because he wasn't paid the right salary to which he felt he deserved, he turned rat. The entire thing went ugly. My dad took his death as a personal responsibility and to the whole of the Monsters, he used it to teach me. That was what Caleb, River, Gael, and myself, always were, a teaching episode.

Our parents didn't truly care, not really. Well,

maybe in some way they did, but it never lasted. Their caring lasted as long as their teaching, or until the next teachable moment. Anyway, the man himself had been chained up. Unlike Caleb's dad, mine liked to prolong the torture of his victims, so he hadn't been fed for nearly a week or given any water. He was dehydrated and starving. His wife, she'd been chained up, given sustenance. At my father's command, I was to shoot her in the leg, in the stomach, in the arms, and then in the head.

I couldn't not follow his command. At the time, I'd been twelve years old.

This was how fucked up our world was.

We didn't have the kind of fathers who wanted to play soccer or go to parent-teacher night. No, our dads taught us how to be killers. None of us had any right being at that school. Being around people, let alone near Emily.

She was good and pure.

The kill she made, that was the anomaly.

My dad had ordered me to shoot that woman, but he'd waited hours between commands. Her husband watched her bleed out. Listened to her sobs and her begs until it finally ended.

"What's wrong with you?"

"Nothing."

"You don't seem to be yourself."

"I'm just not feeling any of this." I shrug.

"You mean the ball?"

"Yeah, the ball, whatever."

Caleb looked around. "You know you can't have these feelings, Vadik. If you do, and they find out, they'll make sure you suffer more. They'll train you more."

I turned to look at one of my best friends. This was why my feelings were so odd. When it came to protecting my boys, I was all over it. No one could hurt them. I guessed when it came to innocents, I wasn't as much of a monster as I thought I was.

"Dude, I'm sitting on a bench keeping out of the fucking way. There's a seamstress waiting to keg me out in a tux. Believe me, I've got no fucking problem with the shit that went down. I'm keeping a low profile." The lies spilled from my lips so easily.

"Wow, sorry."

"You should be. I don't know what the fuck your problem is, but it's got nothing to do with me." I ran my hands down my thighs and stood. "What do you think of this ball?"

"It's our way for our dads to feel out Crane's position."

"You got any more word than the deal he's made for Emily's cherry?" I asked.

"Not a one." Caleb ran his fingers through his hair, looking up toward my dad's big house.

I hated the monstrosity. It wasn't a home.

"What is it?" I asked.

I'd noticed for the past couple of days that Caleb had been acting weird and for me to see it, well, something had to be bothering him.

"Do you know anything about babies?"

"You knock someone up?"

"No."

"Then, no, not a clue."

He reached into his jacket pocket. Anyone else, I'd have snapped his neck from the threat. This wasn't anyone else. This was my best friend. He pulled out a folded-up photo and handed it to me.

I'd seen this many times.

"It's a picture of us when we were kids. What's the problem?" I asked, about to hand it back.

Caleb put his hand against mine and pushed it toward me. "Look at it. I mean really look at it."

Taking a deep breath, I opened my eyes wide and stared at the photograph. Like always, all four of us were together.

"Damn it, Vadik, look at the back."

I flipped the picture over, seeing that this was supposedly taken a few days after we were born.

I looked again at the kid that I knew to be Caleb, and now I wondered. "Why the fuck are you sitting up?" I tilted the picture back to see if he was rested against something, but he wasn't. He was actually sitting up with no support while looking at the three of us.

"Yeah, you tell me how a newborn baby can sit up. I checked it online, it takes months for a newborn to sit up without support."

"What are you getting at?" I asked.

"Something stinks about Dad, about everything." He looked up toward the house.

"My dad has better things to do than to spy on me."

"Oh really, you think he doesn't have a maid or a guard?"

I grabbed Caleb's arm, turned away from the house, and started walking. We left the grounds. I always had a weapon in close reach so no one could stop us or question where we were going.

What we needed was some privacy. I didn't know how far we had to walk to get it, but I kept on moving. We walked down the street and I was accustomed to people crossing the road to get as far away from us as possible. This was what people did. They tried to leave or avoid us.

When we'd put a good distance between my house and any prying eyes, I turned toward him.

"Tell me."

"My dad warned me about Emily. He told me that the four of us couldn't share her, not indefinitely. Our natural instinct would be to compete for her affection. For one of us to want her more than the others. A jealousy."

Shoving my hands in my pockets, I looked at him. I didn't feel jealous that Gael had touched her pussy first, or River had tasted her. I didn't even care that Caleb took her lips either. When it came to Emily, all I cared about was what I'd gotten, and the kiss we'd shared in the bathroom had replayed in my head several times over the past few weeks.

I'd never been jealous of my friends. I didn't care that Gael seemed to find humor in anything, or River's obsession with knives along with his skills. Nor Caleb's natural ability to lead.

They were my friends. My brothers. I had their backs just like they had mine. We were one whole, not four separates.

"What does this have to do about the picture?"

"My dad told me this was what he'd gained from experience. It's clear in this picture I'm the oldest one, Vadik."

"I still don't get what you mean."

"I think there's something in our dads' pasts that binds them all together. What if they had an Emily?" Caleb asked.

"But they've got wives."

"Who they really couldn't give a shit about. Think about the way they treat them."

It wasn't old news that their wives were protected, but in truth, not exactly lovingly embraced by our dads. It wasn't like our fathers were well-known for affection either.

I laughed. "You're turning this into some kind of soap opera."

"I believe our dads were just like us. There's a woman, or was a woman they shared, and I believe I'm the result of that affair."

I looked at Caleb.

He looked exactly like his dad, but with his mother, there was no resemblance.

"You think you're older?"

"Yes."

"What does any of this mean?"

"It means fucking nothing. I don't know what it means exactly."

"You're confusing me right now. Are you trying to prove something or not?" Either way, I wasn't going to stop pursuing Emily. I'd waited too long, and I didn't expect us to go after Emily. She'd been on the edge of our lives for as long as I could remember.

We'd all gone to the same nursery. She'd never gotten close to anyone then either. Through kindergarten, and now up to high school.

She'd been there with all of us.

Only, none of us had made a claim to her, not until she made her presence known with killing to save one of us.

Running fingers through my hair, I looked around. We were at the edge of the town. I saw a couple of curtains twitch and smiled.

"You talked to Gael and River about this?" I asked.

"Not yet. I thought I was losing my mind."

"Come on, let's go and see what they've got to say."

I texted River to find out he was hanging out with Gael in his basement, playing video games. We made our way over, going straight to the basement. Even in Gael's house they were making ball arrangements.

Gael tossed me a beer, which I caught, opening the lid while Caleb got them up to speed. River and Gael studied the picture.

"I don't get what the deal is," Gael said. "So your ass is older than us. Does it matter?"

I took a swig of the beer. It wasn't chilled. I put the can down, leaned forward, pressed my hands together, and waited.

"Yeah, I'm with Gael. I don't give a shit if you're older than us or not. You're still one of us."

"It's not about me being older or not." Caleb ran a hand down his face.

"We've got 'til graduation," I said, imparting that piece of news.

"For what?"

I look toward Caleb who nodded. "For us to have our fun with Emily. His dad gave him a time limit. Come graduation, unless our dads find another reason, she's marrying that tycoon."

"Or she'll be dead," Caleb said. "We all know what happens with traitors. Her life could still be on the line."

This time, Gael stood and kicked the coffee table across the room. The glass smashed.

Seconds passed and a maid came scurrying into the room.

"Fuck off!" Gael yelled the order at her. "No, that shit isn't happening. Your dad actually said this to you?"

He repeated to Gael and River what he'd said to me.

River shook his head. "No, fucking no. I'm not having any of it. There's no fucking way they can do that."

"They can," I said.

"So, it didn't work out for them," Gael said. "Big whoop. I don't give a shit what they say, we're doing what we want. We don't answer to them."

"They're still our fathers. They still have all the control."

"And they can continue to kiss my ass, Caleb. They don't get to win this. We're going to find out what happened," Gael said. "I'm not letting her go to some old asshole with a shriveled dick."

I couldn't have agreed more.

****

Emily

I hated my driver, so seeing him among all four of the Monsters and looking like the grim reaper was on his ass gave me a great deal of satisfaction. He'd made my life a misery.

"I have to take Miss Crane to school," he said.

"What you have to do is go and suck your own dick," Gael said.

I heard the door behind me open and I turned so my back was pressed against the stone railing leading down to the path. My dad looked at me, then at his driver. I saw the displeasure increase when he caught sight of my new friends.

"Hello, Mr. Crane," Caleb said, coming forward. "I hope it's not too much trouble, but we'd like to escort Emily to school today." He looked the epitome of pleasant. I glanced down so he couldn't read my face. I shouldn't be laughing or finding amusement in this.

When the Monsters wanted something, no one could stand in their way.

"It's not appropriate for you to take her," my father said.

I was so going to pay for this. I didn't seem to care. Watching my dad squirm was fun. He rarely was questioned or pushed like this.

"Are you saying we're not good enough to take Emily to school?" Gael asked. "Because from where I stand, you've pretty much said we're scum."

My father's face went a nice shade of puce. "That's not what I said at all."

"I don't know," River said. "I'm starting to feel dirty. I don't like this. If you feel this way, then I'm going to have to tell my father about the way he was raising me. This isn't a good image to have."

This escalated so fast. I looked at Caleb then back at my dad, who smiled.

"I'm sorry, boys. You mistake me. I only mean for you to keep her safe for us. Emily means a great deal to me."

"Oh, we'll also be taking her out for dinner," Caleb said. "We'll have her back at nine-ish. Sound good?"

It wasn't a question, not really. Caleb had already taken my hand. Much to my shame, I shook a little. Fear raced down my back at the gauntlet they'd thrown out. I didn't even dare to look back. If I did, I'd see the threat there and I'd make this day a nightmare, wondering what pain or punishment he had in store for me. There would be a doctor's visit, no doubt about it.

Caleb eased me into the passenger seat of his car. They'd only come in one vehicle. River, Gael, and Vadik were all crammed in the back.

"What the hell was all of that?" I asked, turning to look at them.

"You didn't like how we got you out from your dad's?" River asked.

"I loved it, but you know he is going to make you

all pay."

"I look forward to it," Gael said. "I've already got plans for how I can hurt him. We all know he likes to fuck that art teacher."

"Don't remind me. It's the only reason she's nice to me."

"It's not the only reason," Vadik said. "Regardless of how tough you look, you're nice."

"I'm not nice."

"You saved me. I consider that an act of kindness."

"Next time, do you want me to let them kill you?" I asked.

"Oh, baby, you'd be crying if something was to ever happen to me. We all know you love me the most."

Caleb pulled away from the drive and I smiled, leaning against his plush seats, feeling free for once.

"Thank you," I said. "For coming to get me." I pressed the button on the window, watching it roll down.

I crossed my arms across the window and looked out, basking in the feel of the wind on my face. It felt so good, better than I imagined it would.

Tilting my head back, I took it all in, not wanting to waste a moment.

"You're weird, you know that, right?" Gael said.

"Can we talk about the new girl?" River asked.

I looked toward Caleb, then behind me at the other three. "What about her?"

"We haven't met her. We need to mark her as friend or foe."

"You're talking about Ashley March?" I asked.

"You met her?"

I told them about what happened in the cafeteria.

Gael burst out laughing. "I knew Lauren would react and try to claim her place. Damn, did anyone film it?"

"It's not funny." I didn't like that he laughed at Ashley's gravy episode. No one was allowed to film shit on high school grounds. If they did, it led to punishment.

The crap that happened at Crude Hill High could never, ever get out.

Vadik moved toward my seat, his arms close. His fingers teased my hair. "This new girl. You like her?"

"Yes."

"You want us to be nice to her?"

"She's off-limits for bullying. She's not like any of us," I said. "She's … good."

Gael snorted.

Even Caleb laughed. "There's no such thing as a good person. I heard her mother is nothing more than a whore."

"That's her mother. It doesn't mean she's the same. My dad and brother might have let one of you get shot, but I didn't. I'm different from my family. People can be different from their parents. Or are all four of you the exact replicas of your dads?"

My passionate argument was met with silence.

They all shared a look. It was like they were communicating without saying any actual words, which made me rather jealous. I didn't like it.

"Hey, don't do that. Don't shut me out. You're making my life hell at home because of this. At least let me in on the big secret."

"Your dad's not beating you, is he?" River asked.

I noticed he held his knife in a tighter grip. "No, he hasn't hurt me since he's been warned." I didn't bother to tell them what was going on in his office. The hours spent doing extra studying. Any semblance of a life I had was gone.

Knowing my dad, he'd probably take me out of

high school, not that I cared about that. School sucked, but it was the only reprieve I got at home.

"We'll meet the new girl and make our assessment," Caleb said. "None of us can be held responsible for our parents' sins."

I didn't understand what he was talking about, and in truth, I really didn't care.

The rest of the drive went by in silence. Caleb turned on the radio to some kind of rock station. I didn't exactly hear the words. Music wasn't really my thing. Hearing random people singing about love or hope, or dancing.

I didn't like it.

When we arrived at school grounds, I knew the instant I saw a group formed in a perfect circle that something wasn't right.

Before the car had even parked, I left my bag and pushed my way through the crowd. I shouldn't have been surprised Lauren wouldn't take my warning, but what did shock me was seeing Nancy there. She didn't look happy, but she also wouldn't let Ashley escape.

Ashley, my new friend, her shirt was torn, tears streamed down her cheeks, and I caught sight of the bruise already forming. Blood came from her nose. It didn't look broken. Blood also came from her mouth.

Lauren grabbed Ashley's hair, pulling it tight, making her scream.

Everyone cheered at the violence. Ashley begged for them to stop, but they wouldn't.

She was an innocent. Her mother had made a decision that had landed her daughter in hell.

As I watched her, something clicked inside me.

I'd never fought. Not the punches coming from my dad. I took the beating he made Peter give me. I even meekly sat through my doctor's visits. I hadn't said a word to the driver. My mother left me alone. I was all alone, and not once had I fought back. I'd taken every single little detail that had come my way. No fighting. No nothing.

Ashley had done the same. Her story was different from mine. She wasn't a minion's daughter. Her mother made the choices, and Ashley was the one paying the consequences of them.

I snapped.

When I stepped into the fighting ring, Lauren's back was to me. Just because I'd never been in a fight didn't mean I didn't know what to do.

My knife was back in my bag, but I was strong. I grabbed Lauren's hair, but rather than just give it a threatening tug, I yanked, and I did so hard. She wasn't expecting the attack, and so she let Ashley go, who collapsed to the ground. With my grip still in Lauren's hair, I shove her to the ground, not gently either.

She cried out.

I stood there, panting, waiting.

Lauren flicked her head back and glared right at me. "Really? You're going to fight over this slut?"

"It takes one to know one. I thought I told you to leave her alone."

"You're not the boss of me." She charged me, but I saw it coming, so I dodged it. I was able to land a blow to her stomach, taking her back as she fell to the ground once again, the grass blocking her fall.

The crowd suddenly parted, and one by one, the Monsters arrived. My hands were clenched into fists. I didn't know if I could trust them to take care of this or if I had to keep fighting.

Ashley touched my ankle and I made the decision to give the guys a chance. It was the first time I'd ever done it, but I turned my back on them, letting them all deal with Lauren while I looked at Ashley.

"She's off-limits," River said, his voice carrying.

"Anyone who attacks the new girl will be hurting us, understood?" Caleb asked.

One by one, people dispersed. Not a single teacher came out to help.

I helped Ashley to her feet, holding her against my side. She shook and I glared at everyone. How fucking dare they? I wanted to hurt them. I wanted to kill them all.

"I dare one of you to test our theory," Gael said. "I'm looking to have some fun, and you all know how much I enjoy dishing it out. Just give me a reason."

I didn't linger to see if anyone took him at his word. I held Ashley and walked toward the girls' bathroom.

"So they're the Monsters," she said.

"You heard of them."

"Yeah. I also heard you're their shiny new toy."

I raised my brow at her statement.

"Sorry, it's what they said."

"People are mean."

"Tell me about it. My face turned into a nice punching bag. What is it with that girl? What did I do for her to have it in for me?" She leaned against the counter. I grabbed some tissue and dampened it.

"It's not what you've done. Her own reputation took a beating when she offered herself up to the Monsters not too long ago. She was humiliated. This is her way of getting back in the food chain and not being the scraps along the floor."

"I don't think I'll ever get used to the way you guys talk. High school isn't supposed to be like this."

"It is what it is. You've got to learn to stand up for yourself."

"Before I even knew what was happening, she'd jumped me."

I wiped the blood away. The nosebleed wasn't so bad as it had already stopped. "You're going to have some lovely bruises."

She touched her arm where the shirt was torn. "I don't know why I bother. I ironed the damn thing last night so it looked really good."

"I'd only iron if you got the punch to back it the fuck up," Gael said, coming into the bathroom.

Vadik, Caleb, and River followed him.

"You shouldn't be in here."

"There shouldn't be any more trouble," Caleb said. He put his arm around my waist and kissed my temple.

One by one, all four of the guys did the same.

Ashley's mouth turned into the perfect *O*. "Wait, hold on a second, are you like dating all of these guys?"

"No," I said.

"Yes," all four of the guys said.

Ashley smiled. "Wow, just wow."

"Yeah, you remember that wow, and learn how to look after yourself," Gael said. "If you think it's only Lauren who has it in for you, you've got another thing coming."

"Why?" I asked.

River had my bag and I opened it up, taking out a clean shirt. I was bigger than Ashley, but it would have to do.

"It means she's on the football guys' list to fuck," River said.

I groaned.

"I don't … that's not me."

"Yeah, well, if any of the football team start behaving nice, run the opposite way," I said. I handed her the shirt and pushed her toward the toilet stall.

I didn't know why I wanted to protect her, but for whatever reason, the Monsters were behind me, and for that, I was grateful.

Chapter Twelve

Gael

The new girl was a no one.

Sure, she was pretty and any other time pre-Emily, I'd have fucked her and enjoyed it. I'd have also been in the football guys' position at the helm of humiliating her. Only, I had Emily. The way our girl took care of her, damn it, she turned me on. Taking care of someone shouldn't inspire how turned-on I was getting. It was fucking wrong, but I couldn't help it. Emily had looked like a fierce warrior.

I knew none of my friends had admitted this yet, but I loved her. Fuck, it felt good to think it.

I loved Emily Crane. I'd die for this girl.

Which was why I'd come to the library during Ashley's free period. I'd charmed her schedule out of the receptionist. Not that it had taken much. I scared a lot of people. I had a lot of enemies with what I liked to do for fun. It wasn't my fault women threw themselves at me.

I spotted Ashely's study area. Her bag was left open while there were vultures close by. Damn, this girl had a death wish. This wasn't like any other school and the way she was going, she wouldn't survive an entire month, let alone a term here. She was going to get herself killed.

I walked to the bookshelves, and when I saw my target, I advanced toward her.

She turned with a chemistry book in her hand and a smile on her lips, which quickly turned into a frown when she saw me coming.

Good. I want her afraid of me.

She stepped back.

There was nowhere else for her to go. I had her

surrounded and damn if her fear wasn't pretty.

I put my hands on either side of her head. "What game are you playing?" I asked.

"I-I-I don't know what you mean?" She looked pale, like she was going to throw up.

"You're not stupid. I saw your grades. To the outside world, you have every single right to be here, but I want to know what your game is when it comes to Emily."

She shook her head. Her mouth opening and closing like a damn fish.

"Talk." I snapped my fingers, wanting her to speak so I could move the fuck on.

"I don't know what you're talking about." She still stumbled over her words. "I like Emily."

"Let me get this straight so we're clear, if you hurt her, if anything you do even comes close to touching her, I will fucking kill you. Do you understand?" I asked.

"I don't—"

"Understand?" I wasn't playing. This wasn't a game to me. Emily's safety was my highest priority. Not letting this girl feel safe and warm. I didn't know why Emily cared so much. She didn't answer fast enough for my liking. Wrapping my fingers around her neck, I squeezed just a little.

I wasn't going to kill her. It would be so easy for me to do it. To cut off her oxygen and watch the life drain out of her. I wondered if anyone would really miss her. My parents wouldn't miss me. If anything, my dad would be pissed that all his hard work had been for nothing.

I was his heir. The one to take over his throne.

She panicked and nodded her head.

I let go of her head and she started to pant as if I'd actually attacked her.

"Emily doesn't hear about this," I said.

"I … what is this place?" she asked.

"This is hell. Either learn to play the game, Ashley, or you're going to be just another dead body."

I whistled as I left the library. There was no point for me to return to class, so instead, I went to the art class. I glanced through the window and saw Emily sitting to the side of one of the art boards. I caught sight of Vadik.

After opening the door, I picked up the closest chair, which happened to also have a kid sitting in it, but the force of me taking what I wanted had him falling to the floor with a thump.

"Mr. Parson," the teacher said. "You're not supposed to be in here."

I ignored her and instead sat with my girl.

Emily glanced at me and sighed. "What are you doing?"

"I thought I'd come and hang out with you." I looked at her drawing. It was of a house, with people standing in a field. "That's great, if you're like five years old."

"Do not interfere with her artistic integrity!"

"Go away," I said. "Or we might have no choice but to make it even more public about how you like to fuck parents."

The teacher paled and scampered away.

"Really?" she asked. "That was mean."

"Like you care."

"I don't care, but I also don't need to keep being reminded that there's another spy in my father's camp. He'll know about this."

"If you want, I'll come and make sure he knows to keep a wide berth from you." I winked at her.

Vadik chuckled in the background.

Emily put down her pencil and turned toward me. "What is it?" she asked.

"What? Does there have to be anything? I just wanted to come and see you. Is that a crime?"

"It's not a crime." Her hands lay flat on her thighs. Her gaze traveled around the classroom. "People can watch."

"Let them."

Feeling her come on my fingers, watching her lose control, tasting her lips, it was all I could think about. One time wasn't enough. I'd come to realize, when it came to Emily, nothing was ever enough. I wanted to fuck her so badly, all the damn time.

Not a moment went by when I didn't want her. I craved every single part of her.

Standing up, I cupped her face, tilting her head back.

The classroom, the teacher, the students, all of it faded away until all that remained were me, Emily, and Vadik. My friends never disappeared. I always had them close to me. Never one to let them go.

"Gael," she said. My name was a whimper on her lips, and fuck me if it wasn't the most beautiful sound in the world. I wanted her.

I wasn't gentle as I kissed her. Taking possession of her plump lips, I slid my tongue across her lip. She opened up to me. The moan echoed around me, filling me.

Her hands went to my waist, but I wanted her completely naked. I wanted to feel every inch of her curvy body pressed against mine, and she would be perfect. I wanted her pussy wrapped around my dick, taking every single inch of me as I fucked her hard.

Meeting her tongue, I made do with a single kiss.

Vadik cleared his throat and I knew it was a sign

for me to pull away, which I did, to find most of the classroom had disappeared.

"The bell rang but you were too busy eating her face to care."

Emily glanced over at the teacher and I saw it. The fear of what she would say.

No one made my girl scared. Not a fucking damn person.

I advanced toward the teacher, who already had a cell phone in her hand. I wrapped my fingers around her neck but this time, I didn't go lightly. I didn't make it an idle threat. I slammed the teacher up against the wall, cutting off her air supply. For a few seconds, I didn't even say a word.

Emily called my name, but I didn't hear it.

My only focus was on this woman. This slut.

I counted to ten and I let go, allowing her to get enough air inside before I squeezed again, letting her know without words who held all the power. She choked again, her nails scoring into my flesh, trying to get me to stop, but I didn't. I was the one in control.

I waited again, only this time, I leaned in close. "You speak a single word of what you saw here to her father, and what you've just felt, I will make sure you feel for the rest of your life. I will make it hell. He can't save you. I'm a Monster. It makes me more powerful than him. Your life can be handed to me just so I can have some fun, and believe me, I would love to have some fun with you. You're nothing but a cunt. Do I make myself clear?"

Her head jerked and I smiled.

"Good." I didn't let go and I choked her for a few more seconds, hoping the message would really sink in. She needed to know who the fuck she was dealing with.

After I let her go, she fell to the floor and I loved

to see her at my feet. That was where she belonged.

I stepped away to find Vadik watching me, and Emily with her hands over her mouth. She wasn't crying and for me, I took that as a plus. I grabbed Emily's hand and without another word, I took off.

River and Caleb were outside waiting for us. I nodded toward them but took off with Emily, running in the opposite direction. We'd all be sharing her but there would always be moments when we wanted her to ourselves.

"Gael? What's going on?" she asked, but she didn't pull away. The truth was I didn't want to let her go. At that moment, I'd have put her in my car—if I'd driven to school in one rather than take Caleb's—and drove off with her. Where our pasts meant nothing. I wondered, not for the first time, if she'd be able to handle something like that. Where it was just the two of us. I knew it was what I wanted.

I didn't push it though.

Crashing through the gym doors, I spun her around. At first, she didn't laugh. I'd come to notice Emily rarely had a smile on her face. She never had anything to smile about. We all could relate to that. I certainly could.

There was no music, but I imagined it as I brought her close to me and then spun her around. I did this twice more before holding her and dipping her back in a merry dance.

"What's going on?" she asked, releasing a small smile.

Damn, her whole face lit up, and it took my breath away.

I knew darkness. I'd danced with pain and despair. There had been times as a kid I'd craved affection. When I got older, I fucked women and made them want me just to feel needed, but none of them had come close to the way Emily made me feel.

For once, I felt alive.

I didn't have a death wish.

"What's wrong with just having a little dance?"

"There's no music."

"Then think of a song in your head and dance with me." I didn't let go of her hand as I held her close and moved to tango steps that I'd seen in a movie.

This turned her smile into outright laughter.

Graduation would never be long enough. I knew that now and whatever our dads said, they were wrong. We all could make this work.

****

Emily

Gael's childishness was infectious.

I craved the way he danced around the gym as if he didn't have a care in the world. I wanted to let loose, to not think about what my father would do. He'd kissed me and threatened the teacher. No one had stuck up for me. I knew my art teacher tattled to my dad. All my life, no one was on my side, not even my brother. He'd only ever take care of himself, and in our world, it was the way it worked.

Each day, I grew a little more tired of having to put up with the crap. It wasn't fair. It wasn't right.

Gael spun me around the gym for what felt like an hour. We'd missed class, no doubt. I panted for breath, but he pinned me against the wall. I didn't fight him.

"You're amazing," he said.

"Gael, you don't even know me."

"I know enough."

I shook my head. "Don't." I put my hand on his

chest in an effort to silence him. "You don't know me. You think you do, but that's not possible."

He stroked my hair back, tucking it behind my ear. "You think I don't know you?"

I licked my lips and nodded. "You don't."

"I know you're beautiful."

"Gael, come on. Beauty isn't a good point to have. Lauren's beautiful." I tried to move away but he captured my hands, pressing them above my head, keeping me trapped against the wall.

"You're right. Beauty isn't important, not really. It's a good place to start but not the only part of you I love."

Now my heart started to pound. I couldn't have heard that little detail correctly, could I? No, it wasn't possible. He didn't love me. There was no way he knew love. We barely knew each other.

Yes, we'd grown up together, and I didn't doubt that he had feelings for me, but love? We didn't live in a world where love was allowed.

"You could have let me die. I know you don't mean the shit you say about letting that asshole kill me, but you didn't." He pressed a kiss to my lips and this time, I didn't fight. He ran his nose across my cheek, going to my neck, breathing me in.

I closed my eyes and basked in the touch and feel of him as he surrounded me.

"Fuck, you have no idea how much I want you. You're kind."

"I'm not," I said. I thought about what I did to Lauren today. What I'd thought about most of my peers. I wanted nothing to do with them. It didn't make me a good person. Far from it.

He chuckled. "Compared to me, you are. I've killed."

"So have I." I whispered the words. I didn't think about the man's death. He was nothing.

"You're everything, Emily, and you don't even see it. You put up with so much shit. I saw the bruises and scars. You're a fighter."

This time, tears filled my eyes, and for some reason, I couldn't get them to stop. I felt open, exposed, and I didn't like it.

My throat was tight.

"I think about you all the time. I love the fire in your eyes. The bite of your nails as you hold on to me. I want to see you riding my cock, Emily. I can't wait to see you come. To finally let go of all the bullshit people keep us locked up tight with. You are everything to me. I love you."

He slammed his lips down on mine, his fingers sinking into my hair. This wasn't an act of dominance, but a claiming.

I felt his need pressing against my stomach, but he made no move to touch my tits or pussy. He kissed me like a dying man that only my lips could save.

It was heady and I hated that I couldn't reciprocate.

Years of training kept my words from ever being spoken.

I kissed him back, hoping he got the message with my kiss.

I doubted it. No amount of kissing could take away from the words.

One day, I'd have the guts to tell him, but the sound of a door opening and closing drew him away. He took hold of my hand, and without another word, we were out in the corridor.

The bell had clearly been rung because we followed students to the cafeteria, where River, Caleb, and Vadik were already waiting.

They had a couple of trays and I glanced around the hall, spotting Ashley in the spot I'd been sitting in the last couple of days.

I wasn't going to allow her to be on her own.

Marching over to her table, I grabbed her lunch tray. She looked terrified until she realized it was me holding her tray.

"Emily," she said.

That's right. It's me." I winked at her. "Come on. You don't sit here."

Gael had followed behind me and he took the tray from me.

The cafeteria was silent, watching as he put the tray at the table and moved me to sit opposite my new friend.

I wasn't completely comfortable around Ashley. I still expected her to be a traitor. In our world, you had to expect to be betrayed. It wasn't nice, but this was our reality.

"Wow," Ashley said.

"You keep saying that."

"You've got like four boyfriends," she said.

"No, I don't."

"Yes, she does." Gael kissed my neck.

I rolled my eyes, hating how excited I got at the prospect of belonging to all four of them. I wouldn't give myself even a moment to really enjoy this. I couldn't. I wanted to. The truth was I wanted to give myself to all four of these guys and to hell with the consequences, but with my dad lurking in the background, there was no way I could.

I was trapped.

Feeling sick, I moved my food around my plate, not feeling hungry anymore.

"You okay?" Ashley asked.

"I should ask you the same question. How were your classes?"

"Fine. Even the teachers don't call on me to answer a question. I think I could be completely naked and they wouldn't care."

I saw the tears in Ashley's eyes. Reaching over, I put a hand on top of hers, attempting to offer her comfort but failing miserably. "Don't let it get to you. They're assholes."

"The one thing to remember in all of this," Gael said, pointing some gherkin at us. "They're all in our parents' pocket. Even yours."

"I'm not … my parents…"

"The dude fucking your mom. I don't care. He's paid for them to give you an education."

Ashley's cheeks heated and she looked down at her plate.

"Don't be ashamed of the fact your mother made a deal with whatever devil she wanted to," Gael said. "You've got to make it to graduation and if you keep bowing down like that, you're going to get killed."

"It's not exactly easy." She glanced around the hall. "What if he's one of their dads?" She nibbled on her lip.

"My dad is fucking my art teacher," I said. "Everyone here knows it, but I don't let it get to me." When I found them, I'd been so embarrassed, and I'd been sick. Now, I didn't care. He wasn't even discreet about it.

"Everyone here has secrets. They have a life no one wants you to know about. You've got to learn to fight," Caleb said. "Or you really are going to be eaten alive."

The bell rang. I got to my feet, as did Ashley.

We'd run over for lunch, but Caleb took my hand, pulling me back down to sit.

"What are you doing?" I asked. I seemed to be saying that a lot, but the guys were acting in ways I wasn't exactly accustomed to.

"You're not going anywhere," Caleb said.

"I've got to study."

"Yeah, you can study another time."

"I need your phone number," Ashley said. "I'm going to have to talk to you."

I nodded. I'd never given my cell phone number out to anyone. My dad, brother, and driver were the only ones to know it.

Looking at Caleb and the guys, I felt a tightening in my stomach.

They got to their feet and no one stopped us as we walked out of the school. I couldn't help but glance back, imagining hundreds of eyes watching us.

Caleb opened the passenger door, waiting for me to slide in.

I did.

The guys took the backseat while Caleb got behind the wheel. He turned over the ignition, and I wondered if this was where I find out they'd been playing me all along.

We didn't head out of town but drove toward Caleb's house. There were no other cars. His house was one of the biggest, and as I climbed out of the car, I tilted my head back, looking up at the mansion.

It had to have five floors, and I was sure I saw a guard on the roof.

Caleb put his arm across my shoulders, leading me into his home. Even though there were no cars outside, once inside his house, it was busy.

Manic.

Men and women were running around, carrying cutlery, or vases.

I stayed perfectly still, watching, tucked against Caleb's side.

"What do you think they'd do if I went and melted the ice sculpture?" Gael asked.

"You'd have to deal with your father," a woman said, coming down the stairwell.

This had to be Molly Falls, Caleb's mom.

She offered a smile, coming to stand in front of us. "Boys, you should all be in school."

"Yeah, school sucks, and besides, it's only fair we come and check out how the ball is getting along. We are guests, after all," River said.

Molly looked at the knife in River's hand. "You will not be allowed that at the ball. No weapons."

"You've got to be kidding," Vadik said.

"Your father's rules," she said, turning her gaze toward me. "You must be Emily." She held out her hand and I took it. Her grip was tight, almost like a threat, so I held hers firmly, not showing any weakness.

A minion's daughter I may be, but I had learned not to be trampled over. Molly wanted to dominate, and I got that.

This was her castle. Caleb was her son. She had nothing to fear from me. I had no intention of taking her place.

"I better get back to work." Molly turned on her heel and left.

"Damn, she's as cold as ever," Gael said. "How does your dad put up with her?"

"He pays her in money." Caleb's voice sounded firm, almost angry.

He held my hand and led me out of the house, past the garden and toward the pool house.

"You ever been swimming?" he asked.

"No." Their pool was indoors and as we stepped into the room, I felt the warmth surround me.

"Well, we're going to have to rectify that." He kissed my cheek before wrapping his arms around my waist and throwing me into the pool.

I released a scream, which was swallowed up by the water as I fell into it.

Chapter Thirteen

Caleb

I didn't trust Molly.

There were secrets she knew and she hadn't been honest with me. Every time I looked at her, I had to wonder if she was paid to play the role of my mom. There was no way she gave birth to me.

"What the hell?" Emily coughed as she came to the pool's surface.

I was already removing my clothes, watching her.

"Are you okay?" I asked.

"You're an asshole. A grade-A asshole." She pushed her hair off her face as I stripped down to my boxer briefs.

All of us removed our clothes and one by one, we climbed into the pool, which was deep.

Emily's arms moved out in front of her, keeping her balanced.

From all four directions, we closed in.

There was no way for her to turn. She spun, looking at each of us.

I saw the fear, and we all paused.

"We're not going to hurt you," I said.

"You sure about that?"

"If we were going to hurt you, we'd have done it already," Gael said.

I was the first one to close the distance and wrap my arms around her waist, pulling her close.

She was tense.

"You need to learn to trust."

"It's easy for you guys to say. You've always had each other."

"And now you've got us," River said.

"We haven't given you a reason to be scared of us."

Her heart raced against my palm. With my arms around her, I nodded at Vadik to take care of her shirt. She didn't fight but stayed perfectly still.

"How do I know this isn't a game?" she asked. "What if you want to hurt me, like you've hurt Lauren and so many other girls in the past?"

He tutted. "I think I've proven to you that you're not like other girls. You're special to us."

She rested back against me.

"How is this possible?" she asked. "You know this can't work. All four of you kissing me, touching me, wanting me. You're going to get me killed, or my father."

Vadik got her clothes off, leaving her with only her underwear on.

The curves of her ass pressed against my groin, and fuck me, she was a perfect fit.

"You want us to put a label on it?" I asked, brushing my lips across her neck. Even as her mouth spoke words of dispute about our relationship, her body called to us. Her nipples were already rock-hard, and I wondered if she realized she wriggled against my dick. Her fine ass worked magic as we stood.

"You're all confusing me. I … this can't happen. I know you guys share or whatever. I'm not like that, okay?"

Gael laughed. "All right, let's put a label on it, shall we?"

I didn't let her go, looking over her shoulder, watching my friends.

"The label is simple, you belong to all of us. You're mine. You're Caleb's. You're River's. You're Vadik's. There's no other explanation you need as far as

I'm concerned." He moved in close, his finger tracing down her neck and going toward her breast. He fingered her nipple.

"All four of you?"

"Yes." We spoke in unison.

"And none of you are, like, jealous?"

I leaned down, biting on her neck. "Look at them, Emily. Look at how they watch us. They love to see you in my arms. I know River licked your pussy. That Gael gave you your first orgasm. We don't hate them for it. Knowing you come apart for all of us, that's the fucking dream."

"This is crazy."

"None of us said we were sane," River said.

"Look at the lives we live, Em," Vadik said. "Even you've said so, we don't have a normal life. This is our kind of normal."

They came closer.

I'd loosened my hold on her, but I turned her to face me.

"What about when we're older?" she asked.

"Nothing changes. You're a Monsters' woman. Your life has been claimed by us." The truth was, none of us should be making these claims, not while her life hung in the balance. Not just with her betrothed coming home, but also with her dad's involvement.

"I don't recall agreeing to a party," my dad said, interrupting us.

I look up to see my dad standing at the side of the pool. He wore an expensive designer suit, which he always reserved for business out in the city when he had to appear to look like the leader.

All of our dads worked as a team, united against the rest of the world, but in order for organizations to grow, there had to be a leader. My dad took the role.

Just like I took the role.

I was the leader.

"Emily, your father called me. He wants you home."

She nodded, pulling out of our arms.

My dad was being a cock block. I didn't like it.

No one made to help her as she climbed out of the pool. The uniform she wore was at the bottom of the pool.

"Gael, Vadik, River, go home, boys. Your dads are expecting you."

I realized he never mentioned Mom.

"Molly, take Emily home. Remind Crane about my warning. Understood?"

"Yes, sir."

I frowned as I watched my mother hand Emily some clothes.

My friends had already started to climb out of the pool. They were getting dressed. and I stared at my dad.

"Who is my mom?" I asked.

I'd been determined not to bring this up. Not to take it any further than needed.

My dad, I saw the way he froze. It was subtle but there. He wasn't expecting me to question him.

I waited.

My friends had slowed in their changing to see what my father did.

"Have you eaten?" he asked.

"You're avoiding the question."

"Caleb, you need to be careful what road you go down. I've told you this before."

"And you've stopped us from getting closer to Emily." I moved to the side of the pool, and with one pull, I was out and standing. "You talk, I listen. Those were your rules. They're the ones I've followed. Now tell me what I'm missing." I grabbed a towel, pressing it to my chest.

"What is it you don't want me to know?"

He stared at me and sighed. "Get dressed and come to my office."

Without another backward look, he was done.

"What the fuck?" River asked. "I thought we were going to find out another way."

"I'm tired of waiting. I want to know the truth."

"This is fucked up," Vadik said.

I no longer cared. My dad had never blocked me before, but in the past couple of weeks, whenever I would have gone to Emily after school, he had a job for me. He wanted to distract me.

I needed to know how far these lies went.

I didn't bother with shoes. With my pants and shirt on, I headed to my dad's office. He'd already poured himself a slug of whiskey.

"Come in, close the door, take a seat."

We all did as we were told. Gael was unusually quiet. He hated silences and often filled them with bullshit.

"What I'm about to tell you cannot leave this room. Your dads are aware of what I'm about to disclose."

My dad ran a hand over his face. He was in his late forties, but worked out and kept fit. I knew he was at the top of his game.

I sank into the chair as he pulled out his wallet. He flicked it open and handed me a picture. It was a colored picture, well-worn. There were fold marks, and even some wear from where it has been touched.

"That's Bethany," Daniel said.

I'd never seen a picture of this woman or heard of her name.

I passed it to Vadik, who handed it to River, followed by Gael.

"She's pretty," Gael said, handing it back to my dad.

"I know what you boys think you're doing with Emily. Our Bethany, she was a lot like Emily. A minion's daughter. She wasn't as cautious as your girl. Our woman was a fighter. She called us all out on our shit. Not once did she let us get away with anything."

The moment he started to talk about Bethany, I saw the change in him. This wasn't something he could hide. My dad was in love. "We all loved her. Not one of us cared if it was four of us with her. The moment I saw her with your dads, I didn't care. She belonged to us and I knew all four of us made her happy. Not any one of us could keep her happy, but together, we had her. She was worth fighting for. So we did. We shared her. We left this boarding school fucking shithole behind and carved out a life just for us. She didn't come between the work. Your grandparents couldn't find fault. We were Monsters to the very core. Our loyalty was to each other, to the business, and to Bethany."

He stopped, picked up his whiskey, and took a large gulp. "She … got pregnant. We were all fucking happy about it. Ecstatic. It wasn't planned, as the truth was we shared her enough with each other, let alone a kid, but she was so fucking happy."

I started to feel sick as I knew where this was going to go.

"The pregnancy started out great. She was healthy and everything was going fine. Then, it started with swollen ankles. The pains she'd get. It got ugly and we were later to find out, she went undiagnosed with pre-eclampsia. A risk to both mother and baby. Bethany died giving birth to you, Caleb." Another gulp of whiskey.

This tale was too much for him, I could see it. The pain got to him.

He didn't want to relive it, but for us, he was going to.

"At first, none of us wanted to touch you. You'd killed the love of our lives. The only person who made our lives matter."

I stared at my father and couldn't believe what I was hearing. Sure, it sucked that his woman, their woman, had died, but that wasn't my fault. They were the ones who had the baby, who hadn't used protection. I couldn't even believe I was thinking like this. This wasn't me.

I wanted to hurl abuse at him or do something for him to realize he was fucked up.

"Then one day, I don't know, we'd buried her, and I heard you crying. It was like she spoke to me that day because I knew deep in my heart, you were my son, and I had to go and take care of you. She wouldn't have liked me to leave you out in the dark. So I did. We decided you would need a friend, and that was when they each went and found a woman. Your friends were born nine months later."

"So how old am I really?" I asked. None of what he said was comforting. I'd been living a lie. "And why did you marry Molly if she wasn't really my mom?"

"Your real birthday is on the same day, only you're a year older. Right now, you're nineteen. The rest of you are eighteen. Molly is a means to an end. Our relationship with Bethany was a secret and no one knew any different. We kept her protected. You were ours, and I had to find someone to play the part. She was more than willing, and she knows the score about everything. There's no reason for me to fight with her."

My father stood up. "The only people in this

world you can count on is each other. That's your unit. Do not allow a woman to cloud your mind or to take you from your main goals. Remember, our rules. If her father is found guilty, she, along with her family, will pay for them."

My father nodded at us, turned on his heel, and left.

It was the first time he'd ever been completely honest with me. I didn't know if I liked it.

****

Emily

Caleb's mother was very talkative. She wanted to know everything about me, including how I felt and what my intentions were for her son. I'd never been given the third degree by a mom before. It was odd, but I put up with it because there was no out for me. She'd been sitting beside me, offered me champagne, which I'd declined. There was no way I'd be able to come home drunk. My dad would have been able to find some reason to hurt me, and I always kept my senses.

Before she left, Molly had been sure to pass on the warning Caleb's dad had advised. I wondered if the guys were okay. They looked surprised by him invading their time at the pool.

I pulled back my blankets and climbed into bed, feeling tired. My bedroom door was closed, giving me a false sense of privacy. I wasn't allowed a lock. If my dad wanted to come and hurt me, he didn't want to be hindered.

For the first time since the pain had started, the bruises had begun to fade. My skin was starting to take on its natural color and I also liked not having to deal with the blow of a fist.

A sudden knock on my window made me jump,

and I quickly got to my feet. I'd drawn my curtains closed. I opened them up and saw Caleb outside my window. After flicking the catch open, I pushed the window up.

"What are you doing?" I asked.

"I wanted to come and see you." He climbed into the window.

Stepping back, I waited for him to get inside before I closed the window again. "Are you crazy?"

"Probably. Are you afraid?"

"No, I'm not afraid." I locked the window and turned back toward him.

He wasn't wearing a jacket.

His hand went to my face, tilting my head back. "Do you have any idea how beautiful you are?"

I let him touch me, loving the warmth of his hands on my body. After a few short seconds, I pulled away. "You're going to get into trouble if you're caught here." I moved to my bed, sliding beneath the blankets. Caleb smirked and I had no choice but to move over as he wouldn't budge. He kicked off his boots and slid beneath the blanket.

Lying back against my pillows, I watched him. "What's going on, Caleb?"

"I like hearing my name on your lips."

He looked so lost, and I didn't like that. I didn't know what had caused this sudden change with him, but I wanted to stop it. Reaching out, I put my hand on his cheek. "Tell me what is wrong."

"If you were to die after giving us a child, what would you want us to do?"

I didn't know what to say. I was sure I looked a little crazy as my mouth opened. "What kind of a question is that?"

"A simple one."

"If I got pregnant?"

"Yes."

"And I died?"

"Yes."

Blowing out a breath, I moved away, putting my hand to my head and brushing away some of my hair. "This is all hypothetical, of course, but I'd want you to take care of my baby. No questions asked."

"Even though that spawn had killed you?"

"Especially because it killed me. It's not this imaginary baby's fault, Caleb. You do know I expect all kinds of weird stuff, but this I think goes over the edge of what I can usually understand."

His hand once again landed on my cheek. "I want to get you pregnant."

"Whoa. Not tonight or any other night. I want to at least have a life first, if that's okay with you."

I didn't know where any of this was coming from and I was a little confused. Hurting his feelings wasn't my intention.

"You belong to us, to all of us."

"I still find that surreal."

We both tensed as I heard the sound of boots outside my bedroom door.

Caleb moved and it took a great deal of practice not to burst out laughing. My bedroom door opened and Peter, my brother, stood there.

"Hey," he said.

"Hey."

I wondered if Caleb had thought to move his boots. Sitting up in bed, I turned on the lamp and looked at my brother.

Peter stepped into the room.

I waited, not knowing what to expect.

"Are you looking forward to the party?"

"Not really." That was the truth. Why would I look forward to something like that? "It's a party."

"Did you get your dress?"

"I did."

It was a deep purple that curved around my breasts, molded to my body, and flared out at the hips. There was also a choke collar necklace, which felt more like another brand to the body.

The dress itself wasn't too revealing. It hinted at cleavage, but that was about it.

"You're going to look stunning."

"Isn't that the idea? The reason the Monsters have the party is another way of finding suitable partners." It wasn't lost on me that this was a chance for my dad to finally marry me off. For all I knew, he could be working with the Monsters to get rid of me. I wouldn't put it past him.

My dad was a fucking bastard, used to getting what he wanted. I hated him so fucking much. I wanted him to die.

Clenching my hands into fists, I tried to stem the desire, but it was next to impossible. I didn't know what the guys had done to me, but each day, it was getting harder to just ignore what was happening.

"I want you to know that I am sorry for everything. I … I never wanted to hurt you."

"Are you developing a conscience now?" I asked.

"Em, please."

"Peter, I'm tired. I don't know why you're here, or what you get out of it, but whatever the reason, I don't want to know. I just want you to leave me alone." There was a time I did love my brother. So long ago now.

He'd turned into my father's protégé and that made him less than human in my book. "One day, I hope you can forgive me."

I wouldn't.

I stayed silent.

"You've got to be careful around the Monsters' crew."

"Why? Because they're dangerous? Isn't that a bit hypocritical?"

"I get that you're angry."

"Peter, you haven't known how I've felt for a really long time. If I was you, I wouldn't start to assume." I pretended to yawn, hoping he'd get the message and just leave.

Fortunately, he did.

"I do love you, Emily. I only want what's best for you. I hope one day you can understand that."

The only thing I actually understood right now was that I hated him more than anything else in the world. I stayed silent, waiting for him to leave.

When he did, Caleb appeared.

"Where did you go?" I asked, putting my hand to his chest.

"Under the bed. He's an asshole."

"You don't need to tell me. Believe me, I already know." Taking a deep breath, I forced a smile to my lips. "Sorry you had to hear that."

"I would gladly hear anything for you." He reached out, touching my cheek.

Covering his hand with mine, I craved his touch, the closeness. I needed it.

I closed my eyes and breathed him all in, unable to handle being alone.

"I love you," he said.

His words took me by surprise. I stared up at him, waiting for him to tell me something else, something different. Nothing else fell out of his mouth.

Those were his only words.

Shock rushed down my spine. Gael and now Caleb.

None of this made any sense.

"You don't even know me."

"I know enough. I know who you are."

"Caleb, please."

He stopped me from talking, pushing me to the bed and taking possession of my lips. He nudged the blanket away from me, and I spread my legs, wanting him to surround me.

The hard ridge of his cock pressed against my core, making me melt and moan. This was better than I could imagine.

Caleb lifted himself up but only long enough to start opening my pajama shirt. His palm pressed against my naked flesh. He felt so warm against me. I had no fight. Why would I fight so much pleasure all at once?

It was incredible.

"I bet you're wet for me, aren't you?"

"Please."

He kissed down my neck, going to my chest, then down. His tongue flicking across my nipple. Reaching up, I grabbed hold of the bars of my bed, biting down on my lip to try to keep my pleasured cries quiet. If I gave away too much, we'd both be done for, and I didn't want him to get hurt. His tongue stroked toward my other breast and suddenly, I didn't want to be the only one undressed.

I let go of the bed and cupped his face. He didn't fight me, his lips pressing against mine as I kissed him. This time, I pushed him to the bed and Caleb went willingly.

Straddling his waist, even with my pajama top open, I felt on fire. This was what I wanted, no needed.

With my hands at his shirt, I lift it up and over his

head, throwing it to one side.

"Emily," he said.

My name was soft music from his lips.

He was covered in ink. The Monster mark on his flesh, claiming him to his family and no one else.

I traced my palm down toward where I was straddled. He had more tattoos, but the mark of his family was what drew my attention. Today at the pool, I'd seen they all had matching ink. All on their chest, directly over their heart. I wasn't surprised. Why would I be? This was their future.

"I don't know why you have all changed your mind about me. It scares me."

"Emily, we never changed our mind about you. We all had feelings, but we kept our distance from you. You never showed any interest."

"It's because of what I did for Gael, isn't it?"

"Yes. Until then, we didn't know what you'd do. There are so many people that would kill us and relish in our pain and destruction."

"I'm not one of them."

"We know this now." He ran his hands up my back, going to my shoulders and pushing the shirt off my arms. I didn't stop him. I wanted this.

Climbing off my bed, with my gaze on his, I stood. He had intense blue eyes, darker than the ocean, but so clear. I pushed down my pajama pants, and I wanted to rebel. To not let my father know how he scared me.

If I were to have sex, my pesky virginity would be out of the way, and I'd be clear.

Caleb moved, his legs swinging off the bed. He stood up, and I waited as he removed the last of his clothes.

Together, we were both naked.

I was the first one to move, reaching out, putting my hand on his chest. He cupped my hip, drawing me close. I didn't even hesitate. There was no reason to. We both wanted this. What was the point in fighting it?

As I pressed a kiss to his chest, I heard his sudden intake of breath, and it made me smile.

Trailing kisses down, I had never been so daring in my life. When my intention became clear, he grabbed my arms, holding me steady.

"Emily," he said.

"You keep saying my name."

"You need to know what you're starting."

"I know what I am." With my other hand, I wrapped my fingers around his cock. "Don't you want it?"

"I do. Nothing would give me greater pleasure, but I'd rather you be willing to do this than out of spite because you've seen your brother."

"That's gross."

"But I'm also right."

Caleb moved us toward his bed, and I didn't fight. There was really no point.

Was it because of my brother and his warning? I was tired of Peter thinking he could take the role of protector in my life when he was the furthest thing from it. He had no right to tell me what to do, or how to live.

Caleb lay down on my bed, and I followed him, resting my head on his chest and basking in the feel of him surrounding me. I held on to him, needing his warmth, his closeness, and his love. I had never been loved before, and between the Monsters, they were starting to make me want something I didn't know was possible for me to enjoy.

Chapter Fourteen

Vadik

The rest of the guys were running errands for our dads while I was on babysitting duty. I kept an eye on Emily, who had really taken Ashley under her wing. They were at my place, sitting on the lawn. Sipping at a cup of coffee, I'd noticed something spark within Emily. I liked to see the life within her, the hope. I'd hoped we were helping her to find her backbone, or doing something.

Right now, I didn't think we were being much fun. After Daniel's revelation, Caleb had been a bit uneasy.

He didn't believe he was one of us, which was a load of bullshit. All of what we'd known hadn't changed. We'd been together since birth, and Caleb was just alone for a year before we came along. It didn't change who we were.

My father came out at that moment and sat down.

Marshall Keller was a deadly man. I watched him as his gaze landed on where Emily and Ashley were studying.

"Did you heed Daniel's warning?"

"The girl is a no one," I said.

Ashley was an odd girl. She was too sweet, too kind. Too willing to please. I'd looked into her life, for want of a better description, and I'd stalked her to make sure she wasn't lying. This girl was an anomaly. I read her transcripts from school, checked all social media pages. She used to have a presence before she moved to Crude Hill.

Her life was changed, removed from all that she'd known. I'd feel for her, but her life was by far better.

Even being a mistress's brat, her life was changed. She never had to worry about where the next meal was coming from. The only downside to her existence was that it affected Emily.

She'd never been close to anyone. Even now, Ashley had pulled her close and had decided to paint her nails.

I'd have to do damage control at her dad's.

"Son, I want to give you a warning."

I turned toward my dad. "Why?"

"What we're discovering about Crane, it's not good."

My teeth clenched.

"We haven't confirmed it, but there have been rumors circulating for some time of one of our men desiring our position."

I'd heard of the rumors. "You think he's trying to kill all four of you?"

"We've got evidence he may be the one who sent the MC."

This made me pause. I hadn't forgotten about the MC. Why would I? I looked back toward Emily.

"She didn't know," I said.

"I agree she didn't know, but she's his daughter."

"You've seen the way he treats her. She's nothing to him."

Marshall clicked his tongue. It was then I noticed he held a glass of whiskey. "Never underestimate a woman's value, Vadik. I have taught you better. He treats her like crap, but that doesn't mean he believes in what he's doing. She's valuable."

"No, her virginity is what is valuable."

"Don't hate me for telling you like it is. I'm being honest here. She is certainly causing a bit of a stir, isn't she?"

"Dad, don't kill her."

"You know our rules. There's a reason we keep them in place."

"She hates her dad."

"It's tough."

"What would you have done if Grandpa had threatened to kill Bethany?"

I hadn't spoken to my dad about Daniel's revelation. There was no reason to. He'd loved a woman and she'd died. They'd been able to overcome her death by working together. I got it, but at the same time, I couldn't believe he was talking about killing the woman who now bound their sons even closer together.

Daniel may have the DNA for Caleb, but I knew all four of them saw Caleb as their son.

"Do not speak her name as if you know what it means to love."

"But I do," I said, getting to my feet as my father had already done so to leave. To him, this conversation is over.

"I love her."

"You're a fool."

"Why? You fell in love. You were willing to leave this fucking place to start a family, but I've got to what, marry for the family? Turn my back on love?"

"Bethany was never a threat."

"Neither is Emily. She killed that man. She's not like her father. You cannot do this."

Marshall grabbed my neck, and in the next second, I was pressed against the side of the house. To any onlooker, we were having a conversation, but I knew my father. This was no idle threat.

"Do not cross that line with me, Vadik. We as the Monsters will do what needs to be done. You are not the main demons here, we are." He squeezed even tighter, but I didn't beg. I didn't even try to stop him.

He let me go.

I'd long ago realized that my dad wouldn't kill me. Not his one and only son. I was the only person who could take his place, and keeping the Monsters together meant more to him than any kind of power play.

He turned on his heel and left.

Before I made my way to Emily and Ashley, I gained control of my breathing. The bruise around my neck would add to the list of ones I already possessed.

Stepping off the porch, I walked down to where Emily and Ashley were already packing away their textbooks.

"I have come to the conclusion, Vadik, that you are awesome."

Ashley had thrown her arms around my neck and held me close in a hug. I was about to push her away when she let me go with a huge smile on her face. "Thank you for bringing me here. Your home is so beautiful."

"Are you for real?" I asked.

"Hey, don't be mean. She's giving you a compliment about your house."

"It's not mine." But I couldn't deny how beautiful it was. This was my home.

"I need to go home. Mom's already called. Dinner will be ready in twenty minutes." She nibbled on her lip. "You don't mind driving me?"

"It's why I'm here," I said.

I was willing to allow Emily to have some girl time with her new friend. After I dropped Ashley off, I'd get her all to myself, and that was what I wanted. Grabbing Emily's hand, I pulled her close.

I'd need to talk to the guys about what my father had revealed. There was no doubt Bernard Crane had been caught. He was trying to kill my fathers and take over the Monsters, and there was no way they could let that kind of betrayal slide. Emily's life was on a countdown unless the tycoon proved useful.

Our Emily was slipping through our fingers at a speed I couldn't stand. We'd only just gotten her and already she was being taken away. I couldn't accept it. I loved her. I had never loved anyone in my life, apart from my friends who I considered brothers, but that love was different from my feelings for Emily.

I opened the passenger door for Emily to climb in and let Ashley get in the back. She was still talking about my house. The features she loved the most. I didn't mind her filling the silence.

Emily entertained her.

This happened during the drive toward Ashley's house. We pulled up and I spotted a really nice car waiting in the driveway, which finally silenced Ashley.

"You okay?" Emily asked.

"Yeah, I'm fine. *He's* here."

"Does he scare you?" I asked. I didn't care but I felt the need to ask.

"No. He's a nice guy. I just, don't like him. He's … he's a lot of things and even though my mom knew the score, every single time he leaves, which he does, always, she cries. She's fallen in love with a man she can never have."

Ashely climbed out of the car, but out of the corner of my eye, I'd seen Emily tense the moment she saw the car.

I waited.

"Call me if you can," Ashley said. "We are so doing toenails tomorrow." She slammed the door closed and headed indoors.

"You know who that car belongs to, don't you?"

"Yep." She popped out the *p*.

"Who?"

"My dad." She rolled her head toward me. "That's who."

"Oh."

"Yep. This is news to me. I'm not surprised."

"Do you hate her?"

"Ashley?"

I nodded.

"Hell, no. She doesn't know who my dad is and besides, other than a few greetings, he has nothing to do with her. I do find it interesting, though. You guys looked into her, and not once did you tell me my dad was the one to pay for her."

"His name isn't on the documents."

"No, my driver is, isn't he?"

"Yes."

She blew out a breath. "Whatever. Come on, take me home."

I had no interest in taking her home.

Putting my foot down to the floor, I drove us out of Crude Hill.

"Vadik, what are you doing?"

"You don't need to go home. Not tonight." I was breaking all the rules and I didn't care.

Emily wasn't going home.

Bernard Crane had a lot to answer to, and I'd be damned if Emily paid the price. I should have killed that bastard myself and made it look like an accident. I could do it, no doubt about it. I kept on driving until I saw the sign for a hotel. I had the money. The red glow called to me.

After pulling into the parking lot, I turned off the engine. We'd been driving long enough for the sun to set.

"You okay?" I asked.

"Yeah."

"If you want me to take you home, just say the word."

"No. I don't want to go home." She unbuckled her seatbelt.

We got out of the car and headed toward the main reception where I booked us a room for the night. We didn't encounter any trouble.

The room itself was nice and clean, which was more than I could ask for.

Emily stepped inside and lowered herself to the edge of the bed, checking it. "It feels soft, I think."

I laughed. "Don't be nervous. I'm not going to pounce on you or anything."

"I didn't think you were." She pushed her hair out of her eyes and it was there that I caught the tears.

Going to my knees, I took her hands within mine. "Don't cry. Please don't cry."

"I'm not."

I reach up, swiping the non-tears.

She brushed her face. "I won't cry. I refuse to cry."

"Talk to me."

She pressed her lips together and shook her head. "No, I can't."

"Talk to me, Emily." I wasn't going to give up.

"I'm just, I'm so angry." She pulled her hands from mine and covered her face. "I hate him so much and he can go around and do whatever the hell he wants. It's not fair. I want him to suffer. To feel pain. To know what it's like to be afraid." Her hands clenched into fists.

"I'm here for you."

She dropped her hands away from her face. "You've been so good to me. All of you."

"We're not good people."

"I know that as well."

"But … we all love you, Emily."

"Vadik, please."

"No," I said. I wasn't going to tell her that I loved her. Caleb and Gael had admitted they'd told her. I wasn't going to follow in their footsteps as I didn't think it was right, but now, with everything hanging over our head, there was no choice. She didn't know we were against the clock. Our time together was coming to an end, and I couldn't stand it. "I love you, Emily. I've loved you for a long time. Even with your silly drawings, and your need to constantly have your back against a wall. How cold you are. I love it all. I'm getting to know you and rather than find fault, I see a beautiful, desirable woman. Someone I want more than anything. You're all I could want."

"Vadik?"

I kissed her, knowing she would own my heart for the rest of my life, and I'd gladly give her everything.

****

Emily

My bedroom window overlooked the main drive.

I'd gotten away with spending the night with Vadik as my father hadn't returned home. He hadn't come home for three days, and I took full advantage by being with the four Monsters. The only time I felt alive was when I was with them.

River sat on the hood of his car right now, waiting for me.

I pulled my hair back into a ponytail then grabbed my bag. My driver had lost all control and power over me. He didn't take me anywhere, nor did he do anything. One of my guys did.

Opening my bedside drawer, I paused as I caught

sight of the knife tip. I'd been careless of late. I sat on the edge of the bed and pulled out the knife, holding it up to look at it. This piece of steel had made me feel like I could take from my dad. The tip would pierce my flesh and I'd be free.

The real truth was there was no freedom in taking my life.

My dad could go and do what he pleased, to hell with the consequences, but me, I had to follow all the rules and do as I was told. I hated him just for that reason.

Death wasn't an easy outcome.

I wanted to hurt my dad in every way that mattered.

Rather than put the blade into my drawer, I slid it into my bag and got to my feet.

I was about to leave my room when I caught sight of the man himself in my doorway.

His hands were clenched into fists.

There were so many times over the years that I'd been filled with fear.

Not today.

Not ever again.

He wasn't going to take another moment from me.

"I heard you stayed out overnight," he said.

I stayed silent, looking at him. What woman would fall in love with him? He was evil. I wouldn't even grace him with the title of monster. He wasn't even close to that.

"Tonight, you will come straight home. The doctor will be waiting."

"No," I said.

"Excuse me?"

"I said no. You're not used to hearing that word,

but no. No more beatings. No more exams." I shook my head at him and smiled. "You really are something."

He advanced toward me as if to strike me and I lift my head, refusing to back down. I didn't even flinch as he raised his hand.

"Hit me, I dare you," I said. "You know the rules."

The strike didn't come.

"I see you," I said. "I see the real you, and you're weak. They all know what you're really like. The precious Bernard Crane. The minion. The side story. Does it give you power to move a woman and her daughter here?"

I'd surprised him. Good.

"You think you can talk to me like that? The only reason you're talking back to me is because you believe you can because you've got those assholes."

"Be careful, Dad, those assholes keep you busy." I squared my shoulders. "Tell me, do you beat that woman's teenage daughter?"

His gaze never wavered.

I offered him a smile. "You know, the one interesting thing about you paying for another girl is that she came to that school needing friends, and guess who stepped up for her."

"You will stay away from Ashley."

"What are you doing to try to do, Dad? Fuck the mother until you can groom the daughter into needing you?"

His fingers slid around my neck.

I wished I had the blade in my hand.

"River's right outside." I croaked the words out and he loosened his grip.

"They won't be around forever."

"Until they aren't, you've got to learn to be a

good boy. They're watching you," I said. This wasn't a warning to make him stop, more like a threat I hoped would play out. "And whatever bad deeds you've got going down, they will find out."

Without another backward glance, I left my bedroom. There was nothing inside the room I had to worry about. My neck felt a little tight, but other than that, I was strangely composed.

River stared at me as I climbed into the car.

"What happened?" he asked.

"Nothing."

"That doesn't look like nothing." He saw right through the mask.

"I think I just … I just threatened my dad."

"Why?"

"I don't know. I couldn't hold it back and he pissed me off."

River took off, heading toward the school. I stared out at the town as we passed each house, the streets, and I hated it.

The moment he arrived at campus, I didn't want to go inside. I saw Ashley up ahead, but after confronting my dad, her face was the last I wanted to see.

"Can we get out of here?" I asked, looking at River.

"Sure thing." He hadn't turned the ignition off and in a matter of seconds, we were out of the school and on the road.

"Where do you want to go?" he asked.

"Anywhere that's just not here."

"No destination planned?"

"None."

"Okay."

He didn't stop driving as he pulled out his cell phone and started to text. I didn't complain to him since I wanted this.

When River drove, it was one of the rare occasions he didn't have his knives on him.

"The guys miss you."

"It's still pretty surreal."

"What is?"

"The past few months. I didn't even think you guys knew I existed."

"We knew you existed." He tapped his fingers on the steering wheel.

"I knew you guys did as well. How could I not? You guys were known for keeping order in our school."

He laughed. "Yeah, we have to keep shit together, otherwise, everything crumbles. It's the way it goes." He hummed to himself, a tune I didn't recognize. "What did your dad do for you to confront him?"

"His smug face. I've never let what he does bother me. I get it. He's a guy and all that, but, I don't know. Ashley seems nice and the thought that he brought another woman and her daughter close to us… He makes me so angry."

"Does it make you want to kill?"

I turn to him. "I … that's an odd question."

"I'm an odd kind of guy."

"How many people have you killed?" I asked.

"Do you really want to know the answer to that?"

I paused, contemplating his question, then finally nodded.

"Yeah, I do."

"Then you're an idiot."

"Wow, you really think this is going to get me to warm to you?"

"Emily, I've had your pussy in my mouth. I've got to be pretty fucking special to get a girl like you. I'm just saying."

I couldn't help but laugh. "Wanting to know about the people you killed doesn't make me an idiot."

"I know you think you can take it. How you're some tough woman, but believe me, you're not. You're not even close." He took a deep breath and I watched him. "My first kill, I cried, okay? It affected me. I thought about the life I'd taken. What I'd done. I wasn't ready."

"And now?"

"Now, I kill because I have to. The objective is my main focus."

"And you think that bothers me?"

"Yeah, I do."

"River, I … I didn't cry over that biker guy I killed." I snorted. "I haven't even thought about him. This, right here, right now, this is my very first thought." I shrugged. "What does that make me?"

He glanced at me. "I don't know."

"I think about death." I didn't know why the hell I was telling him this. It wouldn't do. Our lives weren't the same. We were way too different. I was a girl, he was a guy. He stood to inherit an empire built on pain and fear, while I was probably expected to spit out kids like it was a hobby. We weren't alike at all.

"What do you mean?" he asked.

"Death. Dead. No longer breathing."

"You think about killing people?"

"No. I think about … dying." I looked toward him. "I think about what it would be like to end it all." I pressed my lips together. I promised myself I'd never tell a single soul about what I thought about. The knife in my drawer wasn't a prop but an actual chance to take myself out of the game.

"You think about suicide?"

I stayed silent. In my mind, it wasn't killing

myself. "I sometimes just want to be free." I looked at him. "My dad, he's the worst kind of person. I don't want to be under his rule for much longer, and I do think about what it would be like to take that knife and to end his stupid control. I grow tired of the fear. I want an out."

"You can't kill yourself."

"River, don't try to tell me what to do. It never goes down well."

"For everyone else, but I'm not like other guys. I'm different."

I watched him as his gaze stayed on the road. He hadn't stopped once. We weren't going as fast as we had been, but there was a speed to us.

"I know you think I'm not right, but I am. I've been taken. You heard the rumors, the stories. I was so close to death, hours even if I hadn't gotten the medical attention when I did. You've seen the scars. You know what I don't hide. I know what it's like to want to end your own life, but you know what, that was just to numb the pain. To make me feel like I had control."

He slammed his palm against the steering wheel. "I don't accept it. I can't. There's no way I'm going to lie down with this. Those hours, those few days I spent in my enemy's company taught me a lot. It taught me how hated I am but it also made me strong. I will never allow anyone to have any kind of control over me."

"It must be nice to be the one who is in control. You forget, River. I'm just a girl. I don't get to have a say in what I do. My dad holds the cards. I've just got to play his game."

I didn't want to talk anymore.

River took my hand and I didn't look at him even as his lips brushed against my knuckles. "You have so much power, Emily."

Silence filled the car. It wasn't for long. "I know

what the others have told you. I get that it scares you. Four of us."

This time, I had no choice but to look at him. He still had his gaze on the road. Every now and then, he'd stop to look at me. "But I love you too. They may not clearly see that darkness within you, the call of the blade, but I do. Don't end your life because of those assholes. Learn to fight. You've got more power than you realize. All you've got to do is harvest it."

Chapter Fifteen

Gael

The day of the party was alive with activity. This wasn't going to be a small affair. Nearly everyone who was anyone had been invited. This was going to be a huge deal, bigger than even I thought it would be.

To play the part, I'd ordered one of the most expensive designer tuxedos. Emily had already been sent a beautiful purple gown. I'd caught a glimpse of it, snooping in her room. I took great pleasure in getting through Bernard's security. I'd always found odd ways to entertain myself.

"Ah, there you are," my father said, coming into the room.

He was wearing a similar tux but in a gray color.

"I expect you to be on your best behavior."

"When am I not?"

"I mean it, Gael. I don't want a spectacle. You'll be the perfect gentleman."

"And yet you've trained me to be the perfect killer."

He sighed. My father, Dean Parson, was so feared. He'd told me he had a reputation to uphold, which was why he was so hard on me. He wanted me to take over from him, but so people would admire me, not hate me. Personally, I just thought he liked to cause pain. He had a sick and twisted eye for it. He loved to create fear, jealousy. I thought it was why I was a little fucked and got off on other people's misery. Not Emily's, though. I guessed my fascination with her wasn't completely innocent. She was the first person outside of my friends I wanted to care about.

She certainly was the first woman I saw more of

than a damn hole to stick my cock into. I'd shared plenty with my friends. Women were a means to an end, and yes, I could only see us being with one girl. I didn't see us all sharing a bed and being one big harem within her bed. No, I saw us all spending time with her. Emily sharing her time equally with all of us, or not even equally, just whoever was close.

I didn't want her to just fall in love with me. I craved her emotional submission to each of us. She was the first woman to make me feel like that, and I couldn't turn my back on that kind of feeling.

"I've trained you, Gael, to be whatever you're needed to be. You turn the charm on and off when needed, and you know when to strike."

For good measure, he hit me around the back of the head, smooth and swift. It wasn't something I'd forgotten. He knew how to get to me. So many times I'd hit him back that the hits got harder. As I grit my teeth, he smiled. "See, that isn't so bad."

"One day, I'm going to be standing where you are," I said. I didn't know if it was a warning or a threat.

This made my dad smile even wider. "You think I didn't say the same thing to my dad? I know that deep down that he loved me. He wanted what was best for me, and the only way to get what he wanted was to make me hard and strong. I admire that man. I love you, Gael. So damn much it scares me. I will not under any circumstance put you in the ground. Burying you is the last thing I ever want to do."

"Even though I'm not Bethany's?" I asked.

He tensed up but he didn't strike. "There was a time I told the love of my life that I didn't think I was capable of love. She laughed at me. She told me that I was an idiot. I was not only capable of love, but she expected me to love my children. To bring them up in a loving home."

He was sad.

"I try to live with her in mind. That's enough talking about the past." He stepped away from me and I wondered if I was to push a little more, would he strike me? Would he make me bleed?

Tonight wasn't the night. All I wanted was for Emily to be in my arms.

"Is he here?" I asked.

"Who?"

"The guy who has bought her?"

"Yes," Dean said. He poured himself a small shot of whiskey.

"Are you going to tell me what you've decided?" I asked.

"You're still only a son."

"She's the love of my life." I wasn't going to put her life on the line to save face, not with my father. I was a deadly killer who fucked up. "Don't forget without her, you'd have been burying me."

"Don't think I've forgotten that, Gael. I know very much and each meeting I go into, I take that knowledge with me."

"She's ours," I said.

"Gael, go and enjoy the party. You're starting to give me a headache."

"And here I thought we were having a real bonding moment." I rolled my eyes but left the room. I knew when it was best to cut my losses and get the fuck out of there. Today was one of those times.

Clearly, talking about Bethany was tough on my dad.

The moment I stood out in the garden, I paused. All four houses had been opened up for the party. Even though we lived on four corners, there were long pathways that joined up each of the houses. Our space was massive, abundant. There were houses between ours, but they were separated by large brick walls, keeping them in their places.

Caleb said he'd be collecting Emily. I thought about my dad, then about my Emily. I wondered what it would be like to lose her, but also to have to see the baby she gave birth to. Did Dean hate Caleb? Did all of them hate him?

Would I hate any child Emily gave birth to?

I owed her my life.

"Hello."

I turned to see Ashley making her way toward me. She had a sweet smile on her face. I didn't know she'd been invited. She came to stand beside me. "Your home is really pretty."

"What makes you think we're friends?" I asked. A waiter passed us and I took a glass of champagne for myself, nothing for my new little friend.

"Has anyone ever told you how rude you are?" she asked.

"Yes."

"Besides, you can pretend all you want, you like me."

I snorted. "What makes you think that?"

"Emily likes me. I've seen the way you look at her. You can try to believe it's not, but we know the truth. You're in love with her and you won't do anything to upset her." She shrugged. "Don't worry. I'm used to people hating me. You won't be the first person."

"I don't like you."

"Fine by me." She tapped her foot. "So, this is a big deal kind of party?"

"Have you ever been to a party?"

"Of course. I mean, I've been to the usual kind

with a big, bouncy castle and lots of food. Kids running around. I don't see kids."

"Kids aren't invited to these kinds of parties. They make way too much noise." This girl was giving me a headache.

"You seen anyone else?"

"Nope. Me and my mom just arrived."

This was a surprise to me.

"Excuse me."

"Gael, please, don't leave me alone." She stepped to me. "I'm not coming on to you or anything. I'm not flirting. I just, I didn't want to come. My mom made me." She nibbled on her lip.

Sighing, I shook my head but held my arm out for her to grip on to it. "I'm not being nice."

"No, of course not. You're a complete and total asshole. I get it." She nodded. "Did you do any of this?"

"Yeah, totally. I had the time to go hunting for thousands of fairy lights and all that shit."

"Sorry. I guess that was a stupid question, wasn't it? You've got way too much stuff to do than to hang lights and decorate."

"Where did they find you?"

She giggled. "You're not used to me?"

"No, I'm not even close. You're completely opposite from Emily. It's not even funny."

She chuckled. "Sorry. I'm not laughing at you, I promise." She held her hand up but gripped my arm tighter.

This girl pissed me off.

We walked across the lawn and she kept on talking. I didn't know why she felt the need to keep on speaking. I had no interest in what came out of her mouth. There was no reason to stop her even though with her constant noise, she'd started to give me a headache.

"Oh, my God, she's gorgeous."

I'd kept moving but was pulled back as Ashley stood still. Her words caught my attention, and I glanced at her, but she looked across the path, near the bridge. Fairy lights had been hung along either side of the bridge. She stood alone, which I didn't like. but Ashley wasn't wrong.

She looked so beautiful.

The purple dress she wore—I thought was an ugly color—captured my attention. It molded to her curves. Even the short distance away, I saw how it shaped and pushed her tits up, pressing against the front. The strap wrapped around the back of her neck, giving her support. When she turned away, it showed her exposed back.

The bodice of the dress had to be tight enough to keep her tits in. From her tits, it hugged to her hips and then flared out. Her long, blonde locks had been spiraled. The true length made me want to run my fingers through it. Small flowers had been placed in her hair, and when she moved, sparkles came off her.

I wanted her.

"Well, I'd say this is my cue to leave, but go and get her. Don't let her get away." Ashley shoved me toward the woman of my dreams.

I kept on walking, not stopping.

Emily turned and I saw her looking for someone, and then she caught sight of me. Now, when it came to this girl, I knew for a fact, she wasn't the easiest girl to get to smile. Seeing her now, and those eyes, all of it, she made me ache for her in the best kind of way. That smile, all for me, took my breath away.

She moved toward me and I took her into my arms, not caring who saw as I cupped the back of her head and kissed her.

Sliding my tongue across her lips, I captured my woman, kissing her so she knew, without me needing to say words, exactly what I felt.

I stopped the kiss, but I noticed she gripped the lapels of my jacket.

"Wow," she said.

She hadn't pushed me away, nor did she look around to see who saw us.

This was progress. She was like this with all of us.

One day, she wouldn't need to worry. I didn't care what our dads thought was right. If they had any respect for Bethany at all, they'd allow us to keep our woman.

"Hey, you … wow."

She giggled. "You like it? I was so worried. Look at it. It's gross. I like purple but I didn't think it worked as a dress."

"It's stunning. You are, and you have nothing to worry about." I cupped her hip. "Wait until the other guys see you. They're going to lose their minds."

"I haven't seen them."

"Where's Caleb?" I asked.

"I don't know. I waited for him, but my driver ended up dropping me off. The others went before me." She shrugged. "I was worried I'd be turned away at the door."

"Anyone who dared to turn you away will be shot."

This made her smile.

She took my hand, locking our fingers together. "So how about you make my night and dance with me?"

****

Emily

I hoped I was fooling everyone who looked. I wasn't calm or collected. I was fucking terrified. There were so many people here. What startled me was how I saw some politicians, businessmen, but also all the people who made their money in illegal deals. Crooks, criminals, and civilians. It was kind of funny.

This wasn't news to me how the good and evil lived side by side, constantly rubbing together. I guessed I never expected it to be so blatant, but that was what made the best kind of parties.

There were good people here who had no choice but to be in the pockets of those who did the dirty work. This was how it worked.

There was a dancefloor near Caleb's house, and Gael walked me toward it. He'd stopped talking and texted on his phone. I didn't mind the lack of attention. It gave me a chance to look at the beauty.

Even if the party had been thrown by monsters, they certainly knew how to hide their true nature.

So beautiful.

I love fairy lights. They lit up the night sky so perfectly.

Gael cursed and shoved his phone into his pocket.

"What is it?"

"Nothing."

"Gael, don't treat me like I'm a kid."

"Believe me, I don't think of you as a kid."

"Then talk to me."

We arrived at the dance floor, and he pulled me into his arms. Chest to chest. Body to body. We were so close, and it was so perfect. I didn't want to pull away.

"Do you have any idea how perfect you are?" he asked.

"Don't go saying all the right words to get me to shut up. That's not fair."

"But it's true."

I smile. "Come on, don't be that guy who believes you can think better than me. Please? Please?"

"Fine. Fine. They had to go and pick someone up at the airport. Him and Vadik. They'll be here in ten minutes. It's why he couldn't pick you up."

"Where's River?"

"He's also running an errand. He didn't tell me what, but he said he'd be here soon."

"So very vague. Is this what it's going to be like?" I asked. "You guys keeping me in the dark, thinking you can protect me?"

"You deserve to have a good life."

I burst out laughing. "Gael, look around you. I could be killed at Crude Hill High. I don't have a normal life. Out of all of us, the closest person to it is Ashley."

"I've seen her."

"She came?"

"Yes, she didn't want to."

"I know, she told me. Her mom kept saying they weren't going. Then obviously she changed her mind. How is she?"

"Em, you've got to stop playing protector."

"I'm not."

"Do you mind if I cut in?" River asked. His brown hair was slicked back. Even though he wasn't currently holding a knife, I knew one would be on him, if not several.

Gael leaned forward and kissed my cheek. "Of course. I'll go and get us a drink."

Once I was in River's arms, Gael left.

"What's with the frown?"

"Nothing. I'm fine. Where were you?"

"Just running some errands for Dad."

I was growing tired of this. I froze in his arms and

had every intention of pulling away, but he held me firm.

"Don't do that," he said. "I get that you're not happy, but I was organizing a hotel room for a guest. That's all. Nothing dirty. Nothing illegal. Stop worrying."

I stared at him. I don't like to be kept in the dark, not when it came to these guys. "You'd tell me if it was anything to worry about?"

"Yes. You look amazing."

"Thank you."

I leaned forward and rested my head on his chest, breathing in his scent. All four of them smelled a little different. With River, I always felt there was a hint of metal on him. I imagined it was because he always held a blade or was constantly teasing a knife within his grip.

His hands stroked down my back.

I allowed myself to relax. I'd never truly been able to. Not with any of these people. They were all after what they could get. Trying to find a weakness, even in the kids. I knew what it was like to live as a minion's daughter, but I couldn't imagine life as one of their kids. I'd seen the scars that decorated their body. They were worse than mine.

I didn't want to even think about what that meant.

All the hours spent hurting. It made me want to kill, to hurt.

"Can I have this dance?" Vadik asked.

River nodded and placed me in his arms.

Vadik surrounded me. I wasn't used to seeing them so well-kept. They normally wore their uniforms creased and dirty. He pressed a kiss to my cheek. River had already left and I smiled up at Vadik.

"What have you been doing?"

"Nothing."

I sighed. "I know you went and picked someone

up. I know River had arranged some kind of hotel room. Don't do that."

"We're trying to protect you, Emily."

"That's not protecting me. What do you know that I don't?" she asked. "Does this affect me?"

"It affects your father."

I frowned. "What does he have to do with this?"

Vadik sighed and looked around the party. People were staring, but only to admire him. I'd caught sight of some men looking at me, but I didn't care for their stares.

"Your dad has a few deals that our dads are investigating. Certain rumors are running around, and we need to clarify them. This man who has come, he's of particular interest. For Crane to arrange a certain kind of deal, the fact our parents were kept in the dark, it allows suspicion."

Fear traveled down my spine. I wasn't an idiot. I knew what he was saying without saying it.

"Do you suspect he's betraying your families?"

"I don't know, Emily. We all don't know. There's only so much we can find out." He glanced over my shoulder and I followed his gaze to see Caleb nodding toward him. He gave me a smile but then it was gone within the next second.

"Don't go too far. I'll be back." He kissed my cheek and walked away.

I stayed frozen on the dance floor, nerves rushing through my body. I wouldn't put it past my dad to do something so fucking stupid that it would get him killed. I didn't like any of this.

I hated it.

"May I have this dance?" a man said, holding out his hand.

"Sorry, I'm just leaving." I stepped off the dance floor and made my way toward the drinks stand. I didn't go for the alcohol, but I certainly took a large gulp of soda mixed with sparkling water. I didn't know why they had decided to mess up drinks, but whatever.

I felt sick to my stomach.

Something was going on, and I didn't know what, or why, or how. None of it made any sense to me.

I stepped toward the edge of the dance floor, holding my drink, all the time looking in the direction of where Caleb and Vadik had disappeared.

This party unnerved me. Bad things could happen. All it took was the right problem.

I tensed up as I felt someone stand behind me. I went to step away when a hand caught my hip.

"I have to say you're far more ravishing in person than in any of the photos I've seen."

The voice was dark, husky. It didn't belong to any of my guys.

Wait, *my* guys? They didn't belong to me. I had no hold on them.

I tried to move, but the hand lay flat against my stomach, keeping me in place. Years of training about not creating a scene had been instilled in me. All I wanted to do was kick this bastard in the balls. He knew me and yet I didn't know him. I stayed perfectly still.

His finger traced down my arm. "I have to wonder if I should wait until graduation." His lips grazed my shoulder, and I wanted to scream at him to get the fuck off me. "You don't know who I am?"

"No, I don't."

"So you do speak. That's okay. I look forward to hearing you scream my name as I pop that precious cherry I've spent a fortune keeping intact."

"I don't know who the hell you are, but you don't get to have any part of me."

"But that's where you're wrong."

He spun me around and the movement caused me to drop my cup. The man in question was large, muscular in all the right places. He had a scar down his face, but I'd never found them repulsive. He was handsome, but I didn't like him.

"You're so beautiful," he said. "Your dad offered to get you to lose weight, but I like my women with some meat on them." His hand cupped my hip and as I went to go for his balls, he stopped me. The stupid dress didn't help either. "You have no idea who I am?"

"No, I don't."

He put his hands on my back and even as I pressed against his chest, it was useless. I couldn't move. He held all the power. I was so fucking frustrated with all of this, and angry.

"I'm the man who's going to marry you. Your father and I arranged the deal a year ago. You will belong to me, and I do expect you to be a virgin, sweet Emily. I can't wait until I get to pop it."

I stared at him in horror.

My father had sold me to this man.

"I've paid a lot of money for you, and I expect to get it. Until then, this will have to do." He didn't force me to kiss him. His lips brushed against my cheek.

In the next second, he was gone.

I looked around the party, believing I had gone mad, but I knew I hadn't.

I was going to be married.

My body wasn't my own. It was why I was constantly pressed to do those stupid tests. All of it.

Tears filled my eyes, and I felt sick, so ready to vomit.

I moved away from the dance floor, needing space. I had to get away, and so I went toward the tree line, wanting to be so far away from all this falseness that

I couldn't stand.

None of this was real. I needed the fresh air.

The tears slid down my cheeks and I swiped them away. The mascara I wore was supposed to be waterproof. I hoped it was right.

I passed the safety of the party, walking by multiple trees, climbing over a fallen one, and when I came to a stop, I pressed my back against the bark. I took several deep breaths, trying to gain my composure. My heart raced.

River was wrong.

I never had control. It was an illusion.

I was nothing to these people. Just a thing to be bought and sold like I meant nothing. Closing my eyes, I clenched my hands, and hit behind me, impacting the tree. I needed to vent my anger. I didn't have a death wish, not tonight. My first time had already been negotiated. How much was my virginity worth? My sanity? My life? In our world, a life always had a price. What was mine going for?

Chapter Sixteen

Caleb

"You could have asked Emily for a dance before pulling me away," Vadik said.

"There will be time for dancing soon." I grabbed his arm, pulling him away from the party, going to the beach house where we'd get some semblance of quiet. I knew it wouldn't be long before people ended up here and fucked.

These parties were no different than high school ones. Only, the guests were older and appeared far more sophisticated with their champagne and canapes. It was all bullshit.

Gael leaned up against one of the sofas, and River had his blade out and flipped it between his fingers. He'd already cut his finger and blood dripped onto the floor. He showed no sign of pain though. River never did.

Closing the door, I turned toward my friends.

"What's he like?" Gael asked.

"We don't have time to talk about that now. I got confirmation that Bernard Crane hired the MC to take us out."

This had Gael sitting up.

"Our dads know this information and have for a week," I said.

River held the blade in his palm. More blood seeped out, dripping down. "Why haven't they done anything?"

"If Crane organized our murder, then I don't see why they're sitting on their asses. What do we do about Emily? She could be a target," Gael said.

"She will be a target," River said. "The entire family, remember?"

"We can't let her die. I won't let them," Gael said.

I shouldn't have fucking said anything. Gael panicked and all he could think about was going to war. Only, we'd be going to war with the wrong men.

"I don't know why they're holding off, but we've got to deal with this. They've already brought Earl Valentine here. We need to know what they're doing." I had to get my friends to focus. This was the first time our dads could take from us. We'd always been on their sides, and tonight, once I realized the truth, it scared me.

I'd never felt fear before.

"They're playing," Vadik said, and I turned to look at him.

"What?" Gael asked.

"Think about it. They deal in rats and traitors all the time. This is a walk in the park for them. Bernard has become a challenge. One they want to play with."

Gael shook his head. "No. They don't do shit like that."

River laughed. "Come on, it makes sense. Everyone else goes to the cops or tries to steal from them. Crane's got balls. Not only is he making deals behind their backs, but now he's organizing to have their sons killed. This is going to get ugly. We all know it is."

"I don't like this," I said.

"Agreed," Vadik said. "Because no matter which way you look at this, Emily's going to die."

I couldn't stand this. I grabbed the vase nearest me and threw it across the room. I hated Bernard, but I'd hoped my suspicions were wrong. I'd hoped he'd just been a greedy bastard who had seen an opportunity to make some good money using his daughter. This went beyond that.

"What about Ashley and her mother?" River

asked. "Will they be targets as well?"

"They're still news to our dads," I said.

Gael started to laugh. "Are you for fucking real right now?" He ran his fingers through his hair. "There's no way they don't know about her. Don't you fucking see, they know everything. We've got to face the reality here, boys. Our woman, the girl we all fucking love, is going to die and we can't do anything about it. None of us can."

Silence met Gael's words.

I didn't want to accept it, but he was right.

There was no way we could save her. She was gone to us.

River shook his head. "No!" He threw the blade across the room. "I don't. No, we've only just got her. I'm not going to let her go. I can't … we're not going to let her die. She hasn't even fucking lived. She's been trapped and we offered her a life, a chance."

I agreed with River, but right now, I didn't know how we were expected to win this.

"You could be wrong," Vadik said.

"I'm not wrong. Do you think I'd bring this shit to you if I had any doubt? I swear to you, none of this is fake. It's all fucking real." I paced the length of the beach house.

"Then we need to get her out of here," Gael said.

"We'd be the betrayers," River said.

"Our dads can't kill us. Think about it, we're the ones who are set to inherit."

"But they can have more sons," I said, contradicting Gael's theory.

"For fuck's sake, I don't give a shit what you guys are thinking right now. I'm not going to stand by and allow this to happen. I can't." Gael made for the door and I reached out, putting a hand on his arm, stopping him.

Gael could take me.

In fact, I didn't have a fucking clue who was the strongest one out of us all. We were all evenly matched, always had been.

"Ger your hand off me."

"No. I'm not going to let you do anything stupid and believe me, this is stupid."

"I suggest you back away," Gael said.

"Enough!" Vadik's voice echoed around the room. "We are not going to be pulled apart by this. We've come too far."

"There's no way we can let this happen. I'm not letting some old bastard win her over and I'm not going to let her die. I can't."

"None of us are going to willingly let her die." I was insulted that he'd believe I would let that happen. Far fucking from it.

"What exactly are we going to do then? Because from where it looks to me, that's exactly what we're doing."

"Gael's right. We can't let her die," River said.

"I'm not going to let her die."

"We need to know what our dads are working on. We've got to start there." River looked at me. "And you've got to be the one to do it."

"Why me?" I didn't like the way this was going.

"You're the favorite," Vadik said.

"That is such fucking bullshit. None of you know what you're talking about."

"It's the truth," River said. "You're a direct connection to the woman they all loved. Not just one, but all. You have to consider the fact you've always been the favorite."

This time, I laughed, but it was a forced sound. I

pointed at my chest. "I killed her. She died giving birth to me."

"And if that was such a big problem, they'd have killed you already. You need to figure this out."

"Either way, I can't let them take her from me," Gael said. "I won't."

The sudden pounding on the door had us all freezing into place. Some of what we'd threatened could get us killed.

"It's me, guys. Come on, let me in."

It was Ashley.

"What the fuck do you want?" Gael asked, shoving me out of the way to get to the door. He tugged it open with some force.

Ashley's face had lost color. "Er, I think you guys need to go and find Emily. I saw her making for the tree line. She looked upset."

"What?"

"Some guy was talking to her. I don't know his name, but it seemed pretty intimate. I tried to follow her, but I lost sight of her and well, I don't know this area and I figured you guys would know."

"Fuck!" Vadik said. "Earl's talked to her. I bet it's him."

"Split up," I said.

None of us waited. We left the beach house and Ashley followed me.

"No, you stay here."

"I want to help."

"You've helped by letting us know where to look, but you've got to stay here in case anyone asks for us."

"What do I tell them?"

"Lie, think of something."

"But I'm a really bad liar."

"Just fucking do it." I was tired. The others had

already started to look, and I was left behind to deal with our current little problem. I got that Emily had taken her under her wing, but seriously, this girl was so far out of place, it was hilarious.

Heading into the woods, I glanced around. There was only so much light provided from the party.

My father had once said the woods or any forest was a good place to have an accident. A lot of damage could occur and it was all by nature's design. I wasn't interested in what nature could do.

Walking around the trees, I followed the path, not going too deep, but enough for some privacy. If Earl had finally confronted Emily, then there was a chance he'd told her what her father has done, and I didn't think that would have gone down well.

I paused as I heard a sniffle and I turned, catching sight of the purple.

I stepped closer and saw it was Emily and she was hitting the trunk of a tree.

"Emily," I said, capturing her attention.

"Don't you dare," she said.

She pulled away from the tree just as Vadik, Gael, and River arrived. She stormed up to me and I didn't try to stop her as she slapped me hard across the face. I must have deserved it if she was dishing it out.

"You knew, didn't you? All of you." She spun around in a circle. I noticed her hands were bloody from punching the trunk of a tree. I tried to reach for her, but she pulled away. "No," she said. "Don't you touch me."

"Damn it, Emily. Your hand."

"I don't care. You all knew, didn't you? None of you were going to tell me!" She looked at each of us, but we didn't respond. What was there to say? It was the truth. None of us had any intention of telling her everything we knew. It made us the Monsters, but it was the truth.

She shook her head. "Why? Why wouldn't you tell me? Is this your game? A joke? I'm the punch line?"

"No, you're not."

"Then why wouldn't you warn me?" She laughed. "That's why you never went too far, isn't it? You couldn't. You weren't allowed because daddy told you not to." She shook her head. "The fierce Monsters' Crew. The ones who bring death and pain, kept in line by their daddy."

"Emily?"

"No. You're not going to make this better. None of this can ever get any better. This is my life. It's not yours. It's mine. I can't believe…" She stopped and took several deep breaths. "I don't know why I'm surprised. This was way too good to be true. Even your parents are waiting to see if this deal is worth it."

She shook her head. "I can't do this." Her gaze landed on Gael. "You could have at least told me. I saved your life."

She grabbed her dress and took off, heading toward the party. I watched her go, about to follow her.

"I'll go," Vadik said. "She's… I'll make sure she's okay. You've got to find out what shit is going down, and you, keep Earl away from her," he said, pointing at Gael.

"No fucking problem. Do I get to break bones?"

"No, you get to bore the living shit out of him," Vadik said. "And you, tail Crane, see what the fuck is going on."

"Tell her I love her," I said. "I never wanted her to go through this. Never."

Vadik nodded and I had no choice but to watch him leave.

"Do our words matter anymore?" River asked.

"We can't save her. We know this."

"We've got to do what we can." I turned on my heel and decided to go and see my father first. I'd work my way into their confidences, and then I'd save Emily for us.

****

Vadik

Ashley was proving useful for one thing, keeping an eye on Emily. Our girl brushed past her friend, heading into my house. I knew this place like the back of my hand, and so I entered the room and followed the path of dirty shoes. There was already a maid cleaning up the mess.

Partway up the stairs, Emily had taken them off, but I decided to go to the first bedroom. Closing the door, I flicked the lock into place. There was no sign of her, but I heard the water running in the bathroom.

I got to the door and looked inside. Sure enough, there she was.

She was pulling out the flowers that were woven in her hair. She'd also splashed water on her face.

"Emily," I said.

She lifted her head, turning off the tap.

"You didn't need to follow me," she said.

"I did. All of us would follow you. You know that."

"What I do know is that you'll only follow me so far, right? When your dads have given an instruction, I'm on my own."

"It's not like that. We're trying to figure everything out."

She nibbled on her lip and shook her head. "I started to believe everything you said. All of it. Every last little detail, but it's all lies. We can't trust anyone in our world. That's the lie. It's the illusion."

"It's not. You can trust us."

"Then why didn't you tell me?" She screamed the last part. "It's my life. My body. My choice, and I've got none of it." She slapped her chest. "I'm being given to a stranger. I know nothing about him."

I stepped toward her and she backed away. I didn't stop.

Pulling her into my arms, I held her tight, refusing to let her go. "I've got you. This isn't going to happen. He's not going to have you."

She stayed silent and tense.

I stroked my fingers down her back, teasing the strands. "You have to believe we're on your side."

Emily lifted up and she wiped her hands beneath her eyes, removing the tears. She looked at me. Her gaze stayed on mine as she put her hand on my chest.

"You know what they want from me," she said.

I didn't stop her as she reached out, fingering the buttons of my shirt. Placing my hand on top of hers, I reached toward her wrist.

"Emily?" I said.

"What?" She tilted her head back. "This is my life. My body."

"You're making the wrong choice."

"Why am I? He only wants one thing from me and all my life, I've never been given the chance to make this choice. I want to make it now. I need to make it now." She gripped my shirt even tighter. "Please, Vadik. Don't you want me?"

"I do, I want you." There was no doubt in my mind how desperately I wanted her. "This, tonight, I don't know if I should."

"You know I've thought about you," she said.

I still didn't stop her as she began to unbutton my

shirt, but then she suddenly stopped and turned, presenting me her back.

"Help me, please."

Everything told me to stop, but I didn't. I reached out and grabbed the zipper at the back. Slowly, I lowered it down. She'd already removed the strap, and then she stood before me. The bra she wore didn't have any straps and appeared to be fighting to keep it up.

I didn't stop her as she flicked the catch and her tits spilled out. Within seconds, she'd removed her panties, and then she was right in front of me, her hands on my shirt.

My cock was rock-hard.

I should walk out the door and leave her alone. She had to stay a virgin while our parents figured out this deal, but then I couldn't do it. Why would I willingly give her to someone else?

Emily belonged to us.

Her body was ours.

"Don't let them win," she said.

The pain in her voice, I couldn't allow it. Even as I stood frozen, waiting to make a decision, I knew it had already been made for me.

Emily was ours and I was tired of playing by the rules. She didn't want some old bastard pawing at her. She was already claimed as far as I was concerned. We weren't going to let her go.

Grabbing her ass, I lifted her up, but I wasn't going to fuck her in the bathroom. I carried her through to the bedroom. The room was already prepared for any guest who needed to crash. After dropping her to the bed, I stepped back and removed the rest of my clothes. She sat up, watching me.

The bruises on her body had long ago faded, but the scars from previous beatings were still present.

Once I was naked, she reached out toward the light, but I grabbed her hand. "Don't even think about it. I'm not going to fuck you in the dark."

I crawled onto the bed. "You should have picked someone else for your first time. Even Gael would have been better." Pressing her to the bed, I claimed her kiss, nipping at her lips.

She submitted to me as I ran my tongue across her bottom lip, and she opened up to me. I plundered inside, tasting her. She moaned my name and I swallowed it down.

I'd been craving her for a long time. Even before we'd made the decision to have her for ourselves. I'd been watching her for years, even before high school.

I thought by leaving her alone, I was making her life easier, but I'd only put off the inevitable.

Breaking the kiss, I moved to her neck, biting down on her pulse, sucking on her neck.

She cried out and I cupped her tits, pinching the beaded nipples.

"Please," she said.

I knew what she wanted, but she was mine right now, and I wasn't going to let her take control. This was me, and she would do as I wanted, not the other way around.

Traveling down to her tits, I pressed them together, licking those hard nipples. I bit down, and the noises spilling from her mouth echoed around the room. They were what I wanted to hear. Perfect.

She had amazing tits, but I didn't want to leave any part of her untouched.

I kissed down to her cunt, spreading her legs as I did, keeping her open for my mouth. As I put my lips on her pussy, I smelled how wet she was, and I could see it as well. She was ready for my dick, but I couldn't resist a taste of perfection.

Sliding my tongue between her glistening folds, circling her clit, I took it into my mouth and bit down. She arched up, her hand going to my hair, but I wouldn't be stopped.

Devoting my attention to her nub, I flicked, licked, sucked, and bit, driving her wild with need. I didn't let her spill over the edge.

I needed to protect her. Using my fingers on her pussy, I slid them across her slit as I reached into the drawer for a condom. One of the rules of the house was to have condoms in every single room.

After tearing into the packet, I rolled it over my thick prick. Pre-cum was already leaking out of the tip, and I didn't want to get her pregnant, not yet, anyway.

I was a possessive bastard, but first, I had to make life safe for her before a child was involved. It was only fair of us to do so.

With her wriggling on my fingers, I smiled. I hoped she was wet enough to take me. I moved back between those thighs, lined my cock to her virgin entrance.

No one was ever going to claim this again.

As I stared into her eyes, she smiled up at me. "Do it. Please, Vadik, take me."

I didn't need telling again. Gripping her hips, I slammed to the hilt and swallowed down her scream of pain. I'd expected it. She hadn't had a dick inside this pretty pussy, and I was the first one.

I groaned, feeling how tight she is. It had been a long fucking time since I'd been with a woman, and fuck, I was so close to blowing inside her just at the tightness of her cunt. I let go of her hips to hold her hands, locking our fingers together and pressing them to the bed. I was the one with the experience.

I stayed still within her even though the urge to fuck her harder was so fucking intense. All I wanted to do was slam to the hilt within her, fuck her harder, drive her closer to orgasm.

"Fuck, you feel so incredible."

"Then why have you stopped?" she asked, taking me by surprise.

I lifted up to look down at her. "I don't want to hurt you."

"And it's passed. Please, Vadik, please." She arched her hips up and I gritted my teeth at the pleasure.

I held both of her hands above her head, keeping her in place as I moved so I could test just how ready she was to take my cock.

In and out, I used slow strokes, watching for any sign that she didn't want it. She moaned, her eyes closing as I went a little deeper.

Sliding all the way out of her, I thrust inside her, using a lot more force, and she loved it. Her legs circled my waist and I rocked within her, creating a pace that had us both panting for more.

It took every single ounce of control not to come. I wanted to feel her release first.

"Touch yourself," I said.

"Vadik?"

"I did what you asked. I've claimed that cherry. No other bastard is going to know how fucking perfect you are. It's all mine and I'm never giving it back." It was a stupid thing to say because she could never have it back.

I'd cherish this moment forever. Nothing would ever take this away from me. Emily wanted me in her time of need, and I'd come to her.

She lifted her hand and placed it against my cheek. "I'm glad it was you."

I didn't expect her to say those kinds of words. I was in shock, but at the same time, I was so fucking happy. She wanted me and the truth was, I wanted her always.

"Let me see those fingers on that pretty cunt." I kept my dick balls deep within her. She was so tight. I only wished we didn't have a condom between us. I didn't want to feel anything but pure fucking skin, that was all I wanted. Every single part of her. All the time.

She moaned my name, the sound echoing off the walls. The only way tonight would have been better was if she'd actually been in my bed. Tonight could have gone so much better. I fucking loved her more than anything else in the world, and all I could think about was protecting her. I wasn't going to let that old bastard get to her. I'd find a way to keep her. I always would. Not a moment would go by where she'd feel scared or alone. I'd protect and love her. I knew Caleb, River, and Gael would have my back. They only wanted what was best for her as well. It was all we wanted for her.

Nothing else mattered.

She touched her clit, and I stared down, wanting to take it all in. It wasn't the best angle to do this, but it worked, and I got to at least see her. Each stroke over her swollen clit had her pussy tightening around me. So fucking sexy. I couldn't get enough.

"You're going to come all over my dick and when you're finished, I'm going to pound this pussy. Every time you walk, you're going to be thinking of me. Only me."

She arched up, her fingers rubbing her clit, and I watched as the flush built on her skin.

I waited even as my cock just wanted to pound inside her, fuck her harder and completely consume her.

I didn't. I was a good boy and waited for her to

finally come apart in my arms, and when she did, it was a thing of beauty. She completely let go, and the moment her orgasm took over, I completely lost control and fucked her, taking her harder than ever before. I gripped the edge of the headboard and pounded away, taking complete control. Her legs wrapped around me and I just lost it. I took what I'd been longing for, and she just gave it to me, no questions asked.

"Please, please, please!"

I needed to feel her surround me, so I dropped down, wrapped my arms around her, and finished in the condom, kissing her perfectly plump lips and knowing tonight would be one of the best in my life.

Chapter Seventeen

Emily

I wished we could have lingered in the bed, but that wouldn't have done. Vadik removed the condom and disposed of it while I slid back into my dress. He helped me into the zip and I ran my hands down the bodice of my dress.

I wasn't a virgin anymore.

Laughter bubbled out of me.

Vadik kissed my shoulder. "Are you okay?"

"Yeah, I'm fine."

I turned and cupped his face, going onto my tiptoes to kiss him.

"You've got a few crushed flowers in your hair." He reached up and started to remove them.

"Thanks."

"No problem." He dropped them to the floor. "How are you feeling?"

His hand touched my stomach. I grabbed his hand, lifting it to my lips and kissing across the knuckles. "I'm fine." The truth was I was a little sore, but I didn't regret what we'd done. Far from it. Actually, I was so fucking happy. I didn't know how to contain my happiness.

Vadik pushed some hair back. "Come on, let's get you back to the party."

"I don't want to see him again." There was no way I could face the man who claimed to own me. What if he figured out what I'd done? For some odd reason, I wasn't afraid. My dad would kill me. There was no doubt about it in my mind. I was as good as dead. Not only had I lost my virginity, but I also hadn't gotten Vadik to go without protection.

The only way I'd ever be able to be a good daughter in my father's book was if I actually started to use my body to my advantage. Not going to happen. I wasn't interested in Vadik's position as a Monster. All I wanted now was to live my life.

We didn't linger in the bedroom, yet it was the only place I wanted to be. I followed behind Vadik. He held my hand, and I chose not to look in any direction for fear of what any stares would make me feel.

I had to wonder if I had sex written all over my body.

Another woman to have fallen for one of the foursome's charms.

We arrived at the back yard and the music filled the air. Couples still mingled. The party was in full swing.

Glancing across the dance floor, I saw the man who had staked his claim on me and just the sight of him alone made me feel sick. He hadn't caught sight of me, but like a coward, I hid behind Vadik.

"Please, take me home."

"You want to go home?"

"Yes, please."

He glanced through the house. "We'll be detected if I go outside the front. Come on." He started walking, and I kept my gaze down at my feet, following him. The shoes I wore were death traps. The heels were way too big for me, but I kept up with him. We were passing one of the bridges when movement at the tree line caught our attention.

River, Caleb, and Gael were there, but from the looks of it, they didn't want to be known.

Vadik stopped. His hand went tight around mine.

Whatever he'd seen, he didn't like it.

"What is it?" I asked.

He didn't answer, but before I knew it, we were making our way toward that direction.

The houses and beautiful lights fell behind us, and in their place was nothing but the dark woods. For some reason, the lights didn't cast a glow this far inside.

"What the fuck are you doing here?" Caleb said. His words were nothing more than a whisper. Clearly, I wasn't supposed to hear him. His gaze landed on me, then on Vadik.

"What the fuck is going on?"

"You need to take her away," Gael said.

I didn't like this. Any of this. A shiver ran down my spine. There was something they weren't telling me, and I hated them keeping me in the dark. I held on to Vadik's hand a little tighter, not wanting to let him go.

He didn't give anything away, and for that, I was grateful.

A sudden scream filled the air, and I noticed the music had gotten louder. At the party people, were having to get closer to be able to hear themselves talk.

What was going on?

"She has to go," he said.

I didn't pull away, and Vadik held my hand.

"I'm not going anywhere," I said. "If I'm supposed to be one of you, then where I go, you go."

Caleb looked like he wanted to dispute that, but he didn't. He kept his gaze on me, but he wasn't happy.

He nodded his head and then turned on his heel.

I'd fucked up. I knew that.

Vadik didn't let me go as we walked toward the edge of the tree line, and it was there that I saw some of the trees had been taken down to create a rough kind of circle. There wasn't a lot of light but the men who were there held a torch.

Fear slid down my spine as I recognized the man

kneeling on the ground.

He was my brother. Peter.

Blood covered his face. He'd taken a bad beating and the men who surrounded him were all the guys' fathers. I spotted them, and it was Caleb's dad who grabbed his hair tightly and lifted my brother up to his feet.

I'd always felt my brother was tall but looking at him now, he looked like a child.

Tears filled my eyes as Daniel Falls brought the gun to Peter's temple.

They were talking, but I couldn't hear anything. It had all faded away and there was nothing there. Just empty silence.

I couldn't think or feel. It was all a blur, and when the gun went off, Vadik's hand went over my mouth. I didn't realize I'd started to scream.

All four of the guys surrounded me and carried me back to where we came from. At some point, they must have decided I was moving too slow because Vadik threw me over his shoulder and carried me all the way to a car.

I must have stopped crying because I was suddenly pushed into the back seat. Gael moved up behind me, his hand resting on my thigh.

Silence filled the car as they pulled out of the parking lot and started to drive.

The town seemed to blur as we passed everything.

We had to stop driving.

We couldn't keep running.

Peter was dead.

I had just seen my brother get killed. His life had just been taken, and it had all ended so quickly, so finally.

I couldn't believe it.

We hadn't been getting along for so long now. He'd been my father's little protégé and because of that, I'd frozen him out. He so easily followed my father's orders and now, with Peter dead, I knew it was only a matter of time before I followed as well.

"Stop the car," I said.

"I'm not going to do that," Caleb said. Always the one in control, but he couldn't stop this. Not now. Not ever.

"I said stop the fucking car." I dived across Gael, trying the door, getting it open. The car moved left and right, the sudden jerks nearly flinging Gael from the car.

"Stop the fucking car now!" Gael yelled the words and we were brought to a sudden stop.

I crawled over Gael, kicking off my shoes in the process. Falling out of the car, I stopped myself from hitting my face on the hard ground. I panted before finally rising to my feet and staring at these men. The ones who had surrounded me and for the last few months had considered me one of them.

Vadik looked ready to sweep me up off my feet. Gael looked like he wanted to hold me. Caleb and River, both of them stared at me, waiting.

Running fingers through my hair, I looked at all four of them.

"You're keeping something from me. What is it?"

"You need to get in the car, then we're going to take you somewhere where it's safe."

This made me laugh. I couldn't seem to help it. It bubbled up inside me and once I started, I just couldn't stop.

Bending over, I hit my leg as if it was the funniest thing I'd heard him say.

It wasn't.

"There is nowhere safe. Did you just see what happened? He killed my brother at a party."

This wasn't a coincidence.

"I'm not stupid. Don't treat me with kid gloves, and tell me what the hell is going on. I know something isn't quite right and I don't want to keep being left in the dark, now stop doing that."

They all looked at each other, clearly wanting to be anywhere but here right now. Well, tough.

Something had gone down, something big. The death didn't scare me. I'd killed someone with my bare hands. The blood didn't bother me.

No, what got to me was the fact the person they had killed was my brother. Even as I hated him, I still felt responsible for him in an odd way. It was all so fucking messed up. I just couldn't handle this.

"Tell me what is going on."

Caleb looked at his friends and I slapped my hands together. "Stop it. Whatever it is you're thinking right now, it's not working. I know how this shit show runs. I've been living it all my life. They took out Peter. My brother. The party. The sudden interest. The old dude who's supposed to be claiming me and my now nonexistent cherry. I may as well get it all out there for you all to hear. Vadik and I had sex. It was great. I loved every second of it. Now let's move on. Why was my brother killed?"

Tears filled my eyes and I waited for a response.

I looked at each guy in turn, and they kept on staring back. "You know why he was killed, Emily," Caleb said.

The tears fell down my cheeks.

"Then tell me. Use those precious words you love so much."

I was being a bitch. I hated myself, but I couldn't

seem to stop. There was so much anger building inside me. They knew something was going down and they had kept me in the dark. This was big.

"Your father has a very big gray cloud over his head," Caleb said.

"Don't talk in riddles or poetry. Just tell me like it is." I was ready, but deep down, I knew.

"He tried to remove the Monsters, Emily. He wanted to run the show. The deal he struck with Valentine. He didn't consult our parents. He made the deal and tried to keep it quiet. All this time, he's been making underhand deals, and he's also tried to kill us." He pointed at them all.

"The reason he was pissed off with you saving Gael was because he'd organized for the MC to take us out. They were supposed to be the best."

This was news to me. I covered my mouth as I looked toward Gael. "I had no idea."

"We know that."

"You know the rules, Emily," River said, speaking up. He held a knife against his thigh.

I nodded.

Peter was first. One by one, they were going to take us all out.

"But my dad wasn't there," I said. "He didn't witness Peter's death. You all know that removing a family, they do it in one fell swoop. They don't wait around. They don't linger. They just do it." I pressed my lips together. "There has to be a reason they waited."

"Emily," Caleb said, stepping toward me. "Understand this. They are coming for you. They are going to kill you and they will not show a single mercy."

I tilted my head to the side and stared into his eyes.

"What about Ashley?" I asked.

"What the fuck about her? She doesn't matter."

"She's innocent."

It was a lame excuse, but I couldn't run away, not now. I stepped toward him. "Take me back. We've got to see how this plays out."

"Emily, this is fucking stupid," Gael said. "I'm not going to take you back. I'm not going to allow you to risk your life like this. It's fucking suicide!"

"Isn't that what you want?" River asked.

I looked toward him and shook my head. "No, it's not."

"Then why would you go back? You and I both know that you've spoken about the control before. This isn't control. This is fucking messed up."

I moved toward him and put my hand against his chest. "Stop."

"No, you stop. We're not going to take you back so you can fucking die."

"I don't want to fucking die." It was the truth. "What I don't want to do is keep on running and looking behind us. It's no different than how I live now. I don't want this for the rest of my life."

"We'd protect you," River said.

"I get it. I do. I believe all of you, but we're not going to run. I had nothing to do with my dad's betrayal, but I know my house and I could perhaps find something that means your dads won't kill me."

River laughed. "You're fucking crazy. They won't let you live."

"I'm not running." It would be easier to run, now at least. Of course, it would be easy, but it wasn't what I wanted to do. Running now would give us a head start but it wouldn't last. All of us would die when their parents caught up. I didn't want that to happen. Not now. Not ever. "There has to be a way to make this work."

Even as I said the words and the guys shared a look, we all knew I was lying. I was merely putting off the inevitable. Their parents would kill me, but at least I wouldn't have to keep on living in fear.

****

River

Against my better judgment, we took Emily back home, only we didn't let her go home. Instead, I took her to my home. We also agreed to keep Ashley safe. So Ashley was also staying in one of my spare bedrooms while Emily hung out with me.

I don't know why she'd attached herself to this girl, but I wasn't going to argue with her.

After taking a quick shower, the fastest on human record, I made my way back into the bedroom to see Emily standing at my bedroom window. My room always overlooked the yard and the party was still going.

"What is it?" I asked, moving up behind her.

The tears had stopped.

I put my hands on her arms and she leaned back against me. Breathing her in, I couldn't get enough. She was so fucking beautiful. Even now, after a shower, with all the flowers removed from her hair, no makeup, she still was the most precious thing in the world to me.

"I'm just looking down there. Seeing everyone. Drake's just been dragged off and his dad is actually here. I didn't think he came to Crude Hill all that often."

"He doesn't, but Drake's pretty much sent his mother packing."

"I'm not surprised. He thinks he's a gift or something." She sighed. "Look at all of them. Do you think they even realize someone didn't make it home from the party?"

"I don't think any of them care, Em." It would be

rare to find some people who were not completely self-absorbed. This party wasn't one of those occasions. Everyone here had an agenda, some of it was just worse than others.

She stepped back from the window.

The robe she wore had loosened at the waist and I couldn't help but admire the curve of her breast I saw.

Emily watched me.

I untied the rope holding the curtains together and let them fall, giving us both some privacy.

She pushed her hair off her face, and I watched. Entranced by her beauty.

"Do you like what you see?" she asked.

"Yeah, I do."

Her hands went to the belt that gave her a little modesty. My cock twitched and in the next second, I felt myself hardening even more as she opened the robe and let it drop to the floor.

"What about now?"

I saw the scars. They had long since faded now. They shouldn't have been on her flesh, but I didn't care. To me, she was perfect. The scars, the pain, all of it made her feel more real to me.

As I let go of my towel, it fell to the floor so she could see all of me. I'd been taken and scarred. I knew what it felt like to be at the mercy of others, which was probably what she felt like most days.

At everyone else's mercy.

Fucking Vadik was probably the only decision she'd ever really made for herself.

I stood perfectly still as her gaze traveled down my body. I wanted her to look her fill because I was more than happy with the view.

Big tits, rounded hips, juicy thick thighs. She was everything I ever imagined.

That day in the shower wasn't nearly enough time to admire her.

Watching her now, I couldn't help but wrap my fingers around my dick and start to work from the tip and back.

Pre-cum already leaked out of the head, and I rubbed it into my length. "Tell me what you want."

She stepped toward me. She hesitated as she reached out to touch me, but then she covered my grip and I stared at her, waiting. Expecting her to jerk back, the memory of her brother too close, but she did neither.

She touched me like her life depended on it.

Letting go of my dick, I gripped the back of her neck and drew her close. Tilting her head up, I slammed my lips down on hers and claimed her mouth. As I slid my tongue across the seam of her lips, she opened up for me, and I took full advantage, kissing her.

She worked my cock, copying me as I'd worked my length.

I gritted my teeth, feeling the pleasure consume me. There were no other words for how I felt. For my need.

I moved and she followed, not putting up a fight. When I got her to the edge of the bed, I broke the kiss, trailing my lips down her neck and biting on her pulse. Then down to her big tits, licking and sucking at each hard nipple, giving them all of my attention.

Her moans were perfect.

Sliding my tongue across each beaded red tip, I then sucked them into my mouth.

After I pushed her to the bed, she fell back, letting go of my dick. I knelt before her, pressing my hands to her shapely thighs, keeping them spread wide for me.

"This is how I've thought about you. Legs spread,

begging for my cock." Vadik had taken care of her cherry, so I didn't have to go gentle. I didn't want to.

Working her pussy, I took her clit into my mouth, using my teeth to create enough pain that it was probably almost too much, and she screamed my name. The sounds were sweet.

I stroked my fingers up her inner thighs and touched her clit even as I tongued her. I glided my fingers down, teasing across the entrance of her cunt.

No longer innocent.

Just waiting for a big cock to take it.

Pushing two fingers deep inside her, I heard her cry out. Those delicious sounds were everything I wanted.

"Please!"

I stopped licking her.

"That's right, baby, beg me. Let me hear everything you want me to do to you." I went back to feasting on her pussy. She was so fucking sweet. So tasty.

Everything I ever wanted.

This was more addictive than the blade of my knife.

Adding two fingers to her wet cunt, I stretched her out, wanting her soaking when I finally fucked her. It had been so long since I'd been with a woman, and all of them before Emily paled in comparison.

She was all I ever wanted. The only woman I cared about.

My need built and the desire to just fuck her and to say the hell with it was so strong, but I ignored it all, and instead, only focused on her.

On fucking her pussy with my fingers and tongue. Giving her an orgasm so the only sound to come from her lips was the sound of my name. That was all I wanted.

Sliding my fingers in and out of her tight cunt, I watched her thrash on the bed, pressing up against me.

"Please, River, Please."

I pulled my fingers from her pussy, gripped her ass, and ate at her cunt. Tasting her. Licking her. She was so close to the edge, and I wanted to follow her right over but for now, I just needed her to come.

The moment she did, I didn't waste a moment. Once I'd torn into a condom, I slid it over my dick. Rather than enjoy every inch of myself inside her, I slammed to the hilt, feeling the aftershocks of her orgasm as I plunged within her.

Perfect.

I closed my eyes and basked in every part of her.

We were on the edge of the bed and I stared down into her beautiful green eyes. She was looking right back at me.

I didn't move. Just enjoyed the feel of her wrapped around my dick.

I gripped the back of her neck, holding her in place, waiting. I didn't know why I just paused, held in stillness.

These moments, they were important. All of this was about Emily. In our own way, we'd waited for her. We were always willing to let her go, to let her have a life away from us until she took matters into her own hands. The day she killed to protect us, she'd cemented her life with ours. We were all bound together, and I didn't hate that.

I fucking loved it.

So much.

Her hands touched my face, her fingers sinking into my hair, then down toward my ass. As her nails sank into my ass, I knew she was ready.

Smiling down at her, I pulled out of her until only the tip of my dick remained. Then I slammed in, not giving her a chance to get accustomed to my length. I fucked her hard, using the leverage I had on the floor, feeling her tight cunt squeeze me.

Leaning down, I flicked one of her nipples into my mouth and heard her moan. The sounds were everything I wanted.

Her legs wrapped around my waist and I just couldn't control myself. I'd promised myself I'd take my time the first time I made love to Emily. Who was I kidding? There was nothing better than being inside the woman you love.

I was in love with Emily.

She was my soulmate.

My reason for breathing.

Every single part of me wanting her and her alone.

We were destined to be together. I didn't care how fucked up it was. The five of us against the world.

United as one.

"I love you, Emily, so fucking much."

I didn't last. I wanted to, but as I came, I filled the condom, wishing with every breath I took that I'd released into her pussy.

There was no way I wanted to lose her. My desire to bind her to me, to us, was so strong.

The pleasure ebbed away and Emily smiled up at me.

"Are you okay?" I asked.

She nodded. "You don't regret this, do you?"

"No, hell, no. There's no way I'd ever regret being with you." I groaned. "I do have to get rid of the condom."

"Yeah, right. Okay."

"You think there's any chance of getting you on the pill?"

She chuckled. "I'm sure if we talked to my dad, he'd be ecstatic."

I pulled out of her and disappeared into my bathroom. There were knives everywhere. One by the sink, by the bath. I also had them in hidden locations. If anyone was going to hurt me again, they would be in for a surprise.

I disposed of the condom and walked back to the bed to find Emily holding a knife. Freezing into place, I watched her. All kinds of scenarios went off inside my head of what she could do. I didn't want to think of any of them.

The biggest one right now was Emily taking her life. I wouldn't let her die, but if she cut the right part of her body, she'd bleed out. I'd researched this myself to know the best way to attack. Watching her now, I felt fear. I hadn't felt this way in so long.

Emily looked up and smiled. "You know this is dangerous," she said. "It's not good to have knives everywhere. Aren't you worried about people coming in and getting some ideas of attacking you?"

"No one comes into my room." I moved toward her, sliding into the bed beside her and reaching out to take the knife, but she pulled it away.

"I know what you think, but I'm not going to do that. When I do, it'll be at one of your dads' hands."

"Don't say shit like that."

"Why not? We all know it's going to happen."

"Then why didn't you run?"

She ran her finger across the edge of the blade, not next to the tip or in any way that would slice her.

I stared at her finger, mesmerized.

Emily turned to me. "When you were taken, you

didn't hide away. You knew there were monsters out there who would do you harm, right?"

"Yeah, I know."

"If there are people out there who will even do you harm, what hope do I have, River? Sure, I can stab and I can attempt to kill, but I've never been trained. I don't know how to keep myself safe. I'd only be putting off the inevitable and all I've done was hide. All my life that's what I've done. Hid." Tears filled her eyes. "I didn't even know I was going to be sold off to the highest bidder. There have been so many revelations tonight. I don't know how much I can handle right now."

"Emily, we're not going to let you die."

"River. You're not going to be able to save me. None of you are. That's what is going to happen. You can't save me."

I would find a fucking way. I'd only just gotten this girl. I wasn't going to let her go without a fight.

Chapter Eighteen

Emily

River was fast asleep when I woke up. I didn't know how long I sat watching him. He was so handsome. His scars didn't make him ugly. I saw nothing but the beauty he possessed. I wanted to touch him, but I also didn't wish to wake him.

After everything that had happened last night, he needed to sleep. Death would happen.

I knew that now more than ever before. I was going to die. At one of their parents' hands, but rather than be afraid, I was ready.

The last few hours before I died, I had at least gotten to do something I wanted to do.

After sliding out from the bed, I moved toward his drawers and pulled out a pair of sweatpants and a shirt. I was thankful they swamped me. River was bigger than me, taller and more muscular. My stomach growled and rather than linger in the bedroom, I went in search of the kitchen.

Staff were wandering around, cleaning, picking things up, putting the house back to rights. No one paid any attention to me. I had to wonder if this wasn't the first time a strange woman had moved around.

It clearly wasn't a strange occurrence for them.

I found the kitchen and that was where Ashley stood, cooking at the stove. After I cleared my throat, she spun around with a huge smile on her face.

"Can you believe this place? I thought my mom's new place was the bomb but this place is a palace."

I chuckled. "It is big."

"Is this the kind of house you live in?"

"Not even close. No, my house is a lot smaller

than this." I thought of my dad, of what he'd done, and I couldn't help but be angry at him. Not only had he fucked up, but he'd brought Ashley and her mother here as well. They could be in the firing line as well, which really pissed me off. They were innocent.

Two innocent people would pay the price for his greed. Rather than show Ashley this, I kept my smile in place.

I'd learned long ago to play by the rules. It was what I knew how to do. To play the perfect part, even as I had a death sentence hanging over my head. I could do this. I could do all of this.

"You know how to cook?"

"Yeah. When your mom used to work eighteen-hour shifts between two different jobs, you get used to it. You?"

"I wasn't allowed to cook." Even though according to my dad a woman's place was in the kitchen and pregnant. She didn't have brains, and clearly my dad didn't either.

Staring at Ashley's back, I wondered if I should tell her who her stepdad was. I clasped my hands together, feeling a sick feeling in the pit of my stomach.

"Did you have a nice time at the party?" I asked instead. The warning I should be giving her died on my lips.

She chuckled. "Yes. I felt like a princess. I think I stuck out like a sore thumb. I noticed the other women didn't take any of the food that passed them by. Not me, I was so starving and I don't know how they can call those little nibbles food. It's why I came down. River did say to make myself at home, I hope that's okay."

"You do know it's a figure of speech?" I asked.

Her cheeks went a bright red.

"I know, but the cook only gave me fruit and

there is all this food in the fridge."

"I'm only joking around. I don't have the best kind of humor." I ran fingers through my hair. I hadn't even bothered to brush it.

"Are you hungry? Or are you hungover?"

"I didn't drink enough." I probably should have. It would have made my life seem so much easier.

"Me neither. Are you hungry? Don't make me eat all by myself."

"I wouldn't even think of doing such a thing." I winked at her, but what I did need was coffee. "Do you know how to make coffee as well?"

"I'm completely self-sufficient. Always have been. I spent a lot of time on my own, and I'm not looking for sympathy."

"Good, you won't get it." I poured us both a coffee. "Do you take cream or sugar?" I asked, feeling rather domesticated. It was quite fun playing a role. This would be one that wouldn't last.

"Nah, just neat coffee."

"I'm surprised. It's not like you need it." I handed her a cup, which she took while also working the pan of bacon and eggs. I thought I also saw some bagels, toasted, and I even diced-up potatoes. She really was hungry. They were golden brown in the pan on the back. Grabbing a fork, I speared one and took a bite.

They were good.

"You like?" she asked.

I nodded, waving my hand in front of my mouth. "They're also hot."

"Yeah, well, I like to have my food hot and cooked." She winked at me and let out an infectious laugh.

I didn't know if it was because I was going to die soon, or just Ashley and her innocence that had me laughing along with her. Either way, I joined her, loving every second. I sipped at my coffee and rested my head on her shoulder while she cooked. It was comforting just to be in her company.

My stomach growled.

"Take a seat. We're all done."

I sat down in my chair and watched as she served up. She put a full plate in front of me. I wasn't sure if I was going to be able to eat it all, but I'd give it a big go. I was so hungry.

The last meal.

I didn't know when my last day was, but I had a feeling I wasn't going to last long on this earth. How fucking morbid, but there it was. Nothing I could do about it.

I started to eat, enjoying every morsel.

"Is this what you want to do?" I asked.

"Cook?"

"Yeah."

"I don't know. It's probably silly, but I always saw myself as some kind of kitchen goddess. It's lame, I know. I think all those years of waiting for mom to come home. No dad. I decided that when I had a family of my own, I was going to make sure I was prepared for everything." She offered a smile. "You like?"

"You're a good cook."

"Thanks. I like cooking for you."

"You've done it once."

"But I like it." She offered a shrug. "Sorry. I don't want to seem like I'm forcing this or anything. I don't mean to."

I reached over the counter and held out my hand. "You've been a good friend."

"We've only known each other for a couple of weeks. Not really long."

"Long enough to know that you're a good person, Ashley, possibly the best I've ever known." I wasn't lying either. In our world, friends weren't easy to come by. It was one of the reasons Caleb, River, Vadik, and Gael were looked upon with envy. They had each other. Loyalty and friendship were rare commodities in our worlds.

"Em, I'm getting the sense that something is going on. What's happening?"

"Nothing." I forced a smile to my lips, hoping she never knew a moment of pain or fear.

The way she looked over my shoulder, though, I should have known better.

I glanced behind me and caught sight of Daniel Falls. He looked at both of us. First me, then Ashley.

"Hello, Miss. Crane, we meet again." He took in my attire. I hadn't even taken the time to do my hair.

He knew. Without a doubt, I knew what he was thinking.

"I'm sorry for interrupting."

"Not at all," I said, standing.

"Em, you haven't finished breakfast."

"It's fine. I'm full."

"I'm going to be taking Emily with me. I've got something I need to show her."

Today, I was going to die. I'd made it all the way to eighteen, but this was where my time would come to an end.

I wasn't upset or angry.

If I got the chance to see Caleb, Vadik, Gael, and River one more time, I'd tell them how I felt. That way, I could die and probably go to hell with a smile. They would know that in the short time I'd been with them, I'd been the happiest woman alive.

I went to Ashley and hugged her close. "Thank

you," I said.

"I don't like this."

"There's nothing for you to worry about. Okay? You just enjoy your food."

"Should I get River?"

I shook my head. There was really no reason to get him.

Turning my back on Ashley, I felt a little sick, but I looked at Daniel. He was so guarded. It was strange to think that he'd once been a boy much like his son, Caleb. He waited for me to take the lead and each step I took was harder than the last. Sickness swirled within me. The food had been so good, but I didn't want to look like a fool in front of Caleb's dad. It was probably stupid of me to even feel this way.

In and out, I breathed. Hands clenched at my sides.

Time seemed to slow down. With each step I took, in my head, it was like bells were going off. Not a wedding march, but the sound of my doom. The sound of my last moments on this earth.

He didn't lead me into an office or one of the much nicer studies. We came to a door. He twisted the lock, and it opened.

Steps were in front of me.

I could run now.

But I didn't.

One after the other. I started downstairs. There was no light at first. Daniel was close behind me.

The cold seeped into my flesh, making me shiver.

I closed my eyes, not wanting to see or know when the final blow would come. I should have known I'd never be that lucky.

All too soon, the ground slipped beneath my feet and I let out a cry as I landed down into something wet.

Opening my eyes, I saw a light had been turned on, or I'd gone deep enough to where they were waiting. As I looked up, at first, it didn't register what I was seeing. Then, all too soon, a scream fell from my lips.

My mother hung upside down. Her body was naked, but the wound at her neck still dripped.

She was dead.

The wet stuff I'd slipped in was her blood.

My heart raced as I tried to step out of it, but it was everywhere. At my back. In my hair. My hands.

Pulling away from my mother, I came to a stop when I saw my father, only, he wasn't hung upside down.

Knives protruded out of him. One in each shoulder, legs, even his calves. I also saw needles in his face.

He was still alive.

One look at me and I saw the broken man. I had wanted this moment, only now, it came with me.

"It's a pleasure to see you again," Dean Parson said. He had a cloth in his hands. It was stained with blood.

I stared at him, knowing he'd be the one to kill me.

"You don't have a clue what your father or brother did, do you?" Marshall Keller asked.

All of them were here. Even River's father, Ace Block, but he sat in the back, just watching everything.

"My brother?" I asked.

"We know you saw what we did to him," Daniel said with a laugh. "Our sons think we don't know all the tricks there are in the book, but we do. We know a lot more than they can ever imagine."

Licking my dry lips, I looked at each of the men.

None of their soldiers were here.

This was what added to the fear people felt. They didn't use other people to do their dirty work. They relied on no one.

They were the real monsters. No one else.

I stood, covered in my mother's blood. Sickness swirled within my gut, the food I'd eaten only moments ago threatening to come up.

I held it in, waiting, watching, hoping I could find some way to live. But it was all useless.

"Your father has been a very naughty minion," Dean said. "Did you know he's the one responsible for River's kidnapping two years ago?"

This was news to me. "You caught the guy?"

"No, we caught the patsy they'd put in place. I always had a hunch it was someone we knew. I just had to be patient enough to wait for the bastard to get too greedy." Dean approached me, a knife in his hand.

"I regret what I've got to do, Emily. I owe you a favor for saving my son, but I will repay that kindness. I won't give you a slow death. It will be quick."

Tears filled my eyes and I looked at Dean, knowing it was the best I was going to get.

I closed my eyes as I felt the tip of the knife near my throat.

This was it.

I loved four guys and I wasn't going to be able to ever tell them. That was on me.

I hoped one day they would realize that I did love them, in my own way at least.

Taking a deep breath, I waited.

"Stop!"

I opened my eyes, jerking away from the point as I turned to see Caleb, Vadik, Gael, and River in the basement. They were panting as they watched.

I cried out as Dean grabbed me and held the tip of

the blade against my neck.

"Get out of here," I said.

"No," Gael said. "Dad, no. Fucking no. You can't kill her."

A hand covered my mouth, cutting off my air. The sudden swift movement took me by surprise. I couldn't hear what anyone was saying. The world had started to swirl. I couldn't cope. I couldn't breathe.

Just as I thought I was going to die, Dean let me go, but all of a sudden, everything went black.

****

Gael

My relationship with my dad had always been a love-hate one. I hated him but I also loved him. I had pledged my loyalty to the bastard but as I watched him punch the love of my life, if it wasn't for River, Vadik, and Caleb holding me back, I would have killed the bastard with my bare hands.

First, he held a knife to her. Then he punched her.

Emily ended up in a heap on the floor. Completely out cold. I checked to make sure her chest was moving.

Ashley had come running to me the instant Emily had been taken. I'd already been arriving at River's house as she burst through the doors. Caleb and Vadik had arrived next. River was making his way downstairs.

I had never moved so fast before in my life.

There was just no way we could let her die.

The revelation of how deep Bernard Crane's betrayal went even shocked me. She couldn't pay for those sins. There was no way I could let her. She had no right to die because of her father.

"Keep yourself together," Dean said.

He wasn't my dad at that moment. He was my

enemy.

One person I wanted to kill.

"Keep your shit," Caleb said.

Staring at my friend, I breathed in deep and as my friends released me, I stayed perfectly still.

Emily was still on the floor.

"You have him. There's no reason to take her. No reason at all." I slashed my hand through the air.

Emily was covered in blood and each time I looked at her, I feared she was dead.

"You know our rules. She's just a girl. You need to learn not to let a woman have so much control over you. What's done, is done." Dean grabbed the blade of the knife and threw it, using Bernard Crane as a target. The man screamed. I didn't care about him.

I knew for a fact our dads were pissed that he'd been able to operate for a further two years without them even suspecting he was a traitor. He'd been plotting their demise for so long.

They had believed they were invincible.

"What about Bethany?" Caleb asked. "What about my mom?"

They all tensed. I watched it. One by one. Even Ace who sat in the back stood up at her name.

"Don't speak her name," Marshall said.

My dad grabbed a knife out of Bernard and pointed it at Caleb. "You have no right."

"I have every right. I'm her son, aren't I? Her blood runs through my veins. She is part of all of us. Even you. There's no getting away from that. She wouldn't want you to do this. We all know that to be true."

"Boy, I suggest you stay fucking quiet."

The anger in Daniel's voice was clear. I also didn't like how he suddenly had a knife in his hand, waiting to explode.

"We all love Emily. She belongs to us and you can't kill her. Bethany, she'd hate you all for it."

Daniel reacted first, shoving a blade into Caleb's shoulder. It missed his heart, but the threat was there.

"Do not use her here. We have our rules."

Caleb's face was red, tense. This wasn't the first time he'd been stabbed, and it probably wouldn't be the last time.

We'd had to learn to grow up and to do so fast. That was what our fathers always said. There was no room for being children.

"What if it had been Bethany's father? Would you have let her die to pay for his sins? The love of your life."

"Daniel," Dean said.

I noticed my dad had stopped. Even Ace and Marshall were still. They were all watching. They didn't want to kill us. Caleb was their last connection to Bethany.

"A compromise," Ace said, speaking up.

Daniel didn't move but smiled. "A compromise."

"A way for the girl to live and our sons to be … appeased." Ace looked at the ground then at me.

"I know just the thing," Daniel said. "Emily can live. She can live her life without any threat from us."

Caleb nodded but my gut twisted.

"In return, to make sure that there are no repercussions for our generosity to you, you will let her go." Daniel talked slowly. The hint of cruelty in his eyes easy to see.

This wasn't fair.

We all knew it.

"What?" Caleb asked.

"Your girl can live. If you love her enough, if you

really believe she is your Bethany, then to make sure she lives a long and happy life, you will let her go. No more second chances. You take her and dump her. A new identity. A new place, but her name is dead here. She is gone. Died with her traitorous father. That is the only compromise. If you don't agree, Dean here will slit her throat."

"Caleb?" I asked. We couldn't let her go. Not now. We'd only just gotten her, but there was no alternative. I'd rather live knowing she was safe.

"Oh, and the condition, if I ever find out that you went to her, you fuck her, you do anything that makes her real to you, I'll kill her. Her life is now in your and your friends' hands. Tell me, Caleb. You've got a minute to decide."

"Deal," Caleb said.

He held out his hand and Daniel pulled out the knife.

"Ashley as well," I said.

"What?" Caleb asked, as did Daniel.

"If we can't have her. She's going to be alone, Caleb. We can't let her be on her own. Not now. She's going to need someone. Ashley's on their shit list as well. Let her have someone."

Caleb turned back to his father and nodded. "Ashley gets a free pass as well."

Daniel looked back and they all agreed.

A compromise had been met but whatever trust had been there as father and son had been completely severed.

Life, as we knew it, was now fucked beyond all means.

Epilogue

Emily

Something bad had happened. I didn't know how I knew it, but there was a sense of doom lingering in the air.

I couldn't breathe. My throat had closed up.

I jerked awake. My hand went to my neck as I sat up in a bed. I didn't recognize the bed or any of the décor around me. Rubbing at my eyes, I tried to make sense of what I could see, but there was nothing there.

Throwing my blankets off me, I stared down at my hands.

Blood.

There was no blood.

I fell off the bed, landing in a heap on the ground.

The bedroom door flew open and Ashley's arms were around me. At first, I fought against her touch, but then she held on to me, rocking gently.

"It's okay. It's fine. I'm here. I'm with you. You're okay."

This wasn't fucking okay. This couldn't be real.

I knew what I saw. I knew what had happened, and yet here I was, alive. The blade had pressed against my neck. He'd been strangling me, and then everything went dark.

The bastard had knocked me clean out.

Ashley helped me to the edge of the bed. I'd lost so much control, I'd started to cry. "Where are we? What the hell is going on?"

"They told me you'd been out and you would be a little out of it."

"Who? They? You mean Vadik, Caleb, River, and Gael?"

Ashley nodded.

"What's going on?"

"They er, they … they asked me to give you this." She reached into her pocket and pulled out a letter. "I've got to sit with you while you read it."

"A letter?"

"Yes."

I took the letter from her hands. Mine shook.

Weakness. I was tired of feeling weak and I wasn't going to allow myself to feel that way anymore.

Opening the letter, I saw Caleb's writing.

I swiped the tears off my cheek, took a breath, and started to read.

Dear Emily,

You're alive. I know you came here expecting to die, but we couldn't let that happen. We had to know you would live. That you would get to have some semblance of a life. No matter what.

I stopped reading as I just knew this wasn't going to end well.

"Did you read it?" Ashley asked.

"Not yet." I went back in.

Your father's deceit was more than we could even begin to think about. His desire to be number one is what got him killed, and nearly you. None of us want you to die. As you're reading this, you will know Ashley is with you. That is because this letter will be the last correspondence you will ever get. As far as the world is concerned, you died, as did Ashley. Neither of you exists. She has your new passports and identity. You've also got enough money to start over.

You cannot come back.

If you do, you'll die.

We love you, Emily, so much, but we can't let you die.

This is all of us letting you go. None of us want this. We wanted to have a life with you.

I couldn't read anymore. Without going to the bottom, I tore up the letter and let the bits of paper rain down on the bed.

Broken.

They loved me.

They let me go.

"Em?" Ashley asked.

I shook my head. They got to say goodbye and I got nothing. Tears filled my eyes and I tried to control myself. I tried not to be sad, but I couldn't stop.

I was dying inside.

They had let me go so easily. I had to be nothing to them.

"I don't like this. They didn't want you to be upset."

I covered my face with my hands and finally let go. I cried so hard. Ashley's arms wrapped around me, holding me close. This was worse than dying.

"I never got to tell them I loved them," I said.

"I'm sure they knew."

"Do you even know what's going on?" I asked, pulling away.

Ashley turned away and nodded. "Yes. They told me who your father was. I had no idea, Emily, I promise. I … my mom."

Then I realized Ashley was crying.

"Your mom?"

"She's dead." Ashley's tears made a lot of sense now. She'd lost someone. Unlike me, Ashley had loved her mom.

Wrapping my arms around her, I knew I had to be strong. I was never going to see my guys again. They had done much worse than their fathers ever could.

Dean Parson had offered me a clean death. Fast, quick, swift. I hadn't wanted to die, but what Caleb, River, Gael, and Vadik had done, they had offered me only a half-life. They had gotten under my skin, broken into my heart, and they had smashed it into a million pieces. There was no repairing the damage they'd caused.

They had killed me.

I was in love with four men and they had completely broken my heart. I didn't know how I was going to live, but I had to, to make use of this.

Ashley pulled away, wiping at her tears. "Ice cream?"

I nodded. She took my hand, leading me out into the sitting room.

"Where are we?"

She nibbled on her lip and I was even more shocked by what she said next. Not only had they kept me alive, but they had moved me to a different country.

My new name and new life were now in England.

Yay.

To Be Concluded

www.samcrescent.com

MONSTERS' CREW

EVERNIGHT PUBLISHING ®

www.evernightpublishing.com